Silence:
Little Mermaid
Retold

DEMELZA CARLTON

A tale in the Romance a Medieval Fairy Tale series

Lost Plot Press

ISBN-13: 978-0-9922693-3-3

ISBN-10: 0-9922693-3-4

DEDICATION

In memory of those who have met a watery grave.
No man can withstand the ocean, after all.

One

The ocean sang in harmony with the oncoming storm. Though she stood on deck, Margareta could hear the song so clearly she wanted to join in. Three times the captain had tried to persuade her to go below decks, or into his cabin at the very least, but she hadn't budged. As long as a single man stood on deck, so would she.

Besides, the cabin was crowded enough

with the young prince, his entourage and the cloying reek of seasickness.

She smelled it first, before the fine down on her bare forearms stood on end. Then blinding light erupted from the deck, consuming the mast before splashing across the sky. She clapped her hands over her ears, but it did little to quiet the thunderclap when it came.

After that, silence descended on the ship, for the thunderclap had deafened them all.

When the smoking mast cracked into pieces, smashing through the cabin and all those within, no one heard their screams, or the horrible ripping squeal as the ship's beams broke asunder, surrendering to the sea.

While panicked sailors raced around, trying to put out the fires or save themselves, Margareta sat on the deck and calmly removed her shoes and stockings. There wasn't time for more, as the deck was already awash. The ocean licked at her bare toes, enticing her in.

Margareta climbed over the railing, until there was nothing between her and the waves below. She closed her eyes and dropped, feeling the ocean's cold embrace welcoming her home.

It would be so easy to change into a more suitable form for swimming, and let her mermaid instincts take her to depths where no human could follow, but Margareta resisted. She was supposed to be on the surface, not in the sea. She was the daughter of the Master of Beacon Isle, and Beacon Isle was where she belonged right now.

The island was miles away, and it would be a much easier journey in a boat than relying on her own fins. Maybe one of the lighters had survived intact.

Margareta surfaced to survey the wreckage floating amid the waves. A hatch cover, what looked like a cabin door, barrels, corpses, the curve of an overturned boat...

Smiling, Margareta swam for the boat. A well-placed wave set it right way up. All she had to do was climb in and the ocean would take her home.

She had one hand on the gunwale when she clearly heard someone shout, "For God's sake, help me!" before the words ended in a gurgle.

Among the floating corpses was someone who wasn't dead yet, though he would be soon, if no one helped him. He clung to a splintered chunk of mast that rolled in the waves like a drunken sailor. As Margareta watched, it rolled him under the water before bringing him to the surface again, coughing and spluttering.

"Help!"

Margareta did. Guiding the boat to his side, she reached out to haul him in. He was heavier than she expected, though he was the same size as she, and the boat nearly capsized, but water was her element, so Margareta won him from the ocean.

He flopped into the bottom of the boat, the most unlikely catch ever landed. His fine clothes marked him as one of the prince's entourage, but his gasping mouth made him look more like a fish.

"You're just a girl!" he said.

She was far more than just a girl, but Margareta had more important matters to attend to than educating one of the prince's servants. "I'm the girl who saved your life, and I'd have thought you'd have learned better manners as the prince's pageboy."

"Squire," the boy corrected. "I am…I mean, I was…Prince Philip's squire." He was silent for a moment. "They're all dead now, aren't they? He asked me to fetch them some wine, so I was on deck when the mast crashed into the cabin. It must have crushed them instantly."

Margareta surveyed the corpses, then closed her eyes. "Yes, they are all dead. We are the only ones left, and to survive, we must reach the shore. Do you think you can – "

She should have kept her eyes on the ocean, for she knew how treacherous it could be. One moment they were in the boat, the next a wave sent them tumbling back into the water.

Margareta came up cursing. She'd bitten her

lip, so it was with blood on her tongue that she commanded the ocean to do her bidding. The waves brought the boat to her, but the boy was nowhere to be seen. "Find him," she said tersely, ducking under the surface to search for herself.

A glint caught her eye – metal reflecting the lightning above – and she dived, shifting to her tail to give her the power to drag the boy back to the surface. This time, she made the waves lift him into the boat as she hauled herself aboard.

"Take us home," she ordered, and the waves obeyed, parting to form a path before her as a powerful surface current pushed the boat along it.

Satisfied that the ocean would continue to do her bidding without her watching, Margareta turned her attention to the boy. There was no gasping now, nor breathing, either.

"Don't you die on me, squire, or I'll throw you back over the side," she threatened.

No response.

"I saved your life, so it belongs to me, not the ocean. You hear me? No dying on me, now!"

She pounded his chest and back until he coughed up the water he'd swallowed and began to breathe again.

"Who are you?" he croaked out.

"I'm the girl who saved your life," she said again. "So what's your name, squire?"

He mumbled something that Margareta couldn't quite make out, but before she could ask him to repeat it, he fell back against the boards, unconscious. At least he was alive.

Leaving the stormy ocean in her wake, Margareta's vessel sailed for home.

Two

The journey took so long, Margareta stretched out along the bottom of the boat with the boy to get some sleep. She didn't wake until she felt the keel scrape along the sand, and then it was to the bewildering sight of the boy's arms wrapped around her, as she embraced him. She only had a moment to reflect on it, before a wave tipped the boat over on its side and they both tumbled out onto the wet sand.

The wave retreated faster than it had advanced, taking the boat with it.

Margareta considered for a moment, then let the sea have its fun. She had no further need of the boat, for she was back at Beacon Isle. She felt refreshed by her swim and short voyage, but the boy looked the worse for wear. That he was still unconscious worried her. She dragged him further up the beach, out of reach of the playful waves, but still he didn't rouse. Perhaps he had been injured. The surgeon in Harbour Town would know what to do.

She rose, straightened her salt-dampened gown, and marched up to her father's house. Pausing only to ask a maid to have some water sent up to her chamber so that she might wash, Margareta headed for her father's chamber, where she was certain he would be at this time of the morning.

"Good morning, Father," she greeted the Master of Beacon Isle. "We have a man on the beach in need of medical attention. A boy, really, but he claimed to be the prince's squire before he nearly drowned."

"Good morning, Margareta. I — " Father

broke off to peer at her. "I thought the *Golden Eagle* wasn't due back in port until tomorrow. I didn't hear it return."

"And you won't," Margareta said bluntly. "It was more of a wallowing duck than any kind of eagle. The stupid captain sailed her into a storm and she sank."

Father sighed. "Margareta, what have I said about sinking ships? I realise it is your nature, but – "

"It wasn't me!" she protested. "I haven't sunk a ship in my life! I told the captain about the storm, but he didn't listen. Lightning struck the mast and it exploded into flaming pieces. There was little I could do but return home."

"What of the prince? The captain and his crew?"

Margareta sighed with genuine regret. "Dead. All dead. Except for the boy I left on the beach, of course. If he survives. Can you send a surgeon down there, please, and some strong men to carry him to the house?"

"What, aren't you going to carry him up

here yourself? You've played the knight in shining armour, rescuing him and all. Let him play the swooning princess while you carry him up to your chambers to seduce him." Father grinned as though he'd made the best joke.

Margareta frowned. "I don't intend to seduce him. The boy nearly died. You must think me a monster, Father, if you believe I would do such a thing. I…I'm going to wash, and change into fresh things that aren't encrusted in salt. Please have someone see to the boy." Not waiting for her father's response, she swept out of the solar.

<h1 style="text-align:center">Three</h1>

Erik drifted, dreaming of a mermaid who had saved him. A few times, he could have sworn he felt her in his arms, like one of the sirens in the stories. But sirens lured men to their deaths, just as mermaids dragged mariners to the depths of the sea. He'd never heard a tale about one who saved people.

When he awoke alone on the sand, he was disappointed. Oh, not that he wasn't dead — that he was quite relieved about, or he would be, once he worked out where the mermaid had gone.

Perhaps she had only left to get her sisters, and together they would finish him off.

"Is he dead?" a male voice asked.

Erik leaped to his feet. He found himself face to face with three fishermen, their arms full of fishing nets. "Prince Philip is dead," he said.

One of the men shrugged. "Don't know any princes. But dead men don't talk or jump, so I'd say he's not dead."

"He looked dead," one of the others said.

"Maybe he's like that miracle man who came back to life," the third ventured eagerly.

Erik didn't feel like a miracle man, nor did he deserve it, if Philip was dead and he yet lived. "Is there a town nearby? Or somewhere I might find a ship? I must go home to tell the king about Prince Philip."

"Up that way, just over the dune," the first man said, pointing. "White Harbour always has some ships coming and going."

Erik thanked them and trudged toward what

turned out to be a sizeable town, clustered around a busy harbour that he recognised as the one at Beacon Isle. Could it really have been less than a week since he sailed out of this very harbour?

He enquired at the docks, and soon found a vessel willing to carry him and his ill tidings home, though for a price.

"Do you have any coin to pay for the passage, boy?" the captain asked, squinting at him.

Erik reached for his belt, where he still carried Philip's purse. He had coin enough to pay for the passage of their entire party home, but he knew better than to say so. "Will two silvers buy me a cabin on a ship that sails on the next tide?" he asked innocently, showing the captain his two coins while palming a third.

"The next tide?" The captain's eyes widened. "I had not thought to leave until the morrow. Rounding up the crew, loading the cargo…these things take time. But for three silver coins, I might manage it." He held out his hand a little too eagerly for Erik's liking.

Erik sighed and counted the coins mournfully into the captain's outstretched hand. "Very well. Show me to my cabin."

The cabin the captain ushered him into was barely big enough to hold a bed, but Erik didn't care. He stretched out on the pallet and stared at the wooden ceiling, wishing he wasn't the one who would have to tell his parents that their favourite son was dead. Maybe that's why the mermaid had spared him: she knew a worse fate awaited him if he lived.

All too soon, the ship cast off, and he felt the lull of the waves once more. Erik surrendered to sleep, only to dream of a mermaid who rocked him in her arms.

Four

When she was dry and dressed, Margareta returned to the beach where she'd left the boy. She was surprised to find no one but a few fishermen mending their nets, like they normally did in the afternoon. Her father had heard her, after all, she marvelled.

But when she asked the servants which guest quarters he'd been given, no one could tell her anything. It was as though none of them had yet seen him. Her father would know, she was sure of it, so Margareta marched back to her father's solar to ask him.

She found him bowed over the desk, with his head in his hands.

"What's wrong, Father?" she asked. "Is he dead?"

He glanced up. "Who?"

"The boy on the beach." Margareta wished she'd thought to ask the squire's name.

"I know nothing of any boy, except my own. And they have flown." He sighed heavily. "Something terrible has happened to your brothers."

Margareta clutched the table so hard her knuckles went white. "What happened? They're not dead, are they?"

He shook his head. "No, but they may as well be. While they were hunting, they met a witch, who took offence at some imagined slight. Before they could stop her, she cursed them. All of them. She turned them into birds and made them fly far away."

Knowing her brothers, the slight was probably not imagined, Margareta knew, but she didn't say. For all her reputation for seduction as a siren, even the most chaste of her brothers could boast more romantic conquests than she. Most likely one of them had made a coarse comment, and the others had joined in, until she cursed them all.

"Is there a way the curse can be broken? Did you speak to the witch? Perhaps – " she began.

Father silenced her with a wave of his hand. "She presented herself right here in my solar, and told me she would never lift the curse. But the curse could be lifted by a maiden who loved my boys enough to make a huge sacrifice for them." He reached for her hand. "Margareta, I know you like to save people. Here is your chance. Do you love your brothers?"

She might not like them at times, but… "Yes, I love them," she said steadily.

"Are you willing to make sacrifices to save them?"

Margareta hesitated, before she finally said,

"What kind of sacrifices?"

"She said they could be saved in one of two ways. If each of them could persuade one woman to declare her love and dedicate her life to one of your brothers, a dozen girls in the same night, they might break the curse themselves."

Margareta burst out laughing. "If my brothers – all twelve of them – agreed to get married at all, let alone on the same night, to women who truly loved them…Father, that would be a greater miracle than raising a man from the dead. If that is their only chance, then my brothers are truly lost."

"There is another way."

She managed to stop laughing. "There had better be, or they shall be birds forever."

His grip tightened around her fingers. "If one maiden is willing to sacrifice her voice for as long as it takes to break the curse, they will be set free. She cannot speak or laugh or even whisper."

"One maiden. That would be me, I imagine?

You wish me to be silent for…how long, exactly?"

He shook his head. "I do not know. Weeks. Months. Maybe even years. Until the witch believes you have sacrificed enough to make her lift the curse and restore my sons to me."

"Father, find someone else. I must find the boy. He was unconscious, and needed help. I can't find him if I can't ask anyone about him."

Father captured her other hand, squeezing both in a desperate entreaty. "Margareta, my darling Meg, there is no one else. If you love me, as you love your brothers, you will do this. Save them. I will find a place for you in the priory, and tell them you have taken a vow of silence. You can roam through the rose garden, or spend all day in the library, or do whatever you please, as long as you do it in silence. I beg you to save your brothers."

The library and the rose garden were her two favourite places on the island, as her father knew well. It would mean staying longer on land, too, without returning to the ocean where instinct might take over and make a monster of her as it had so many of her mother's kind. She needed very little persuasion when he offered her such things. But… "What of the boy?" she asked sharply. She needed to know he was safe.

"I will find him, and make sure he is safe. If you will save my sons, my heirs."

Margareta took a deep breath. "All right, Father. I will do it. Silence my voice to save my brothers."

"Thank you!" He threw his arms around her, hugging her as he hadn't since she was a child.

And from that moment, not a sound passed her lips. For her father was right about one thing. If she chose to save someone – be it her brothers from some folly or some nameless squire from a shipwreck – she would not rest until she had succeeded.

Five

For a week, Margareta wandered through the house and the priory like a corporeal ghost. She avoided people she would normally acknowledge, taking her meals alone in her chambers. If it weren't for the library and the rose garden, she would have been bored out of her mind.

All right, she was ready to scream when a thin wail erupted from the other end of the rose garden. Curiosity got the better of her, so Margareta crossed the courtyard to investigate.

The wail issued from a bundle of blankets held tightly to a young woman's breast. The woman herself reclined on a bed of sorts, and she was wrapped in more blankets than her baby.

"Lady Margareta!" the nun exclaimed before dropping a deep curtsey. "Lady Margareta is the Master's daughter. She has taken a vow of silence, in the hope that her sacrifice will persuade the Lord to save her brothers."

Margareta opened her mouth to correct the woman, then remembered and closed it again.

"My lady, may I present Lady Penelope, widow to the late but valiant Sir Godfrey, who died defending the priory?"

Margareta inclined her head. She hadn't heard of any such knight, but if the baby in Lady Penelope's arms was his, he couldn't have died very long ago.

The nun fluttered her hands. "Oh, but you wouldn't have heard about Sir Godfrey's brave deeds, for you had not yet arrived. Lady Penelope, you must tell her."

It was Penelope's turn to duck her head. "Perhaps when I am recovered. I am but recently widowed and I fear the birth of my daughter…"

The nun's hands fluttered more violently. "But of course. Perhaps I should help you inside, so that you can rest?"

Penelope wrinkled her nose. "I much prefer it out here. I'm sure you have better things to do than hover around me all the time. I will be perfectly well here for a while, if Lady Margareta does not mind sharing her garden?"

For all that she wanted to be alone, Margareta knew she would look churlish if she refused. Besides, she was curious about the other woman. And she wanted a peek at the baby.

So Margareta smiled, spreading her arms wide to signify how delighted she was to share the garden her father had planted for her.

As if on cue, a bell tolled.

"Oh! That is the bell for prayers. I must go!" The nun hurried away.

When Margareta was sure the nun was out of earshot, Penelope said, "If you wish me gone, merely nod and I will ask them to take me somewhere else tomorrow. It is so different to things at home. There, I would have a private courtyard where I could sit and my sleeping chamber is just for sleeping. Here…why, the moment I arrived and they found out I was with child, they confined me to a dark room and seemed terrified that some dark spirit might harm me or the baby if a single ray of sunlight or a breath of fresh air reached us. I threatened to walk out here by myself if they did not let me out of that room."

Margareta felt a strong desire never to have children. Not that her father was likely to accept any offer of marriage that came her way, anyway. That would mean giving her a dowry and part of the island, which he would already have to divide between his twelve sons. Of course, that only strengthened her desire to hold Penelope's child, for if she could never have one of her own…

Margareta held out her arms for the baby.

Penelope looked surprised. "You want to hold her? Sure." She settled the baby in Margareta's arms and sat back. "Her name is Melitta."

Margareta stared at the sleeping child. She weighed next to nothing, yet Melitta held more power over her than the tiny girl would ever know. The aura of magic that swirled around her marked her as a witch. Magic followed bloodlines, which meant her mother might also have some magical talent. Or it could have come from her father, though it was rare for magical ability to manifest in men.

"My husband was a fool," Penelope said. At Margareta's startled glance, she smiled, revealing a spot of blood on her lip from where she'd bitten it to cast what Margareta could only guess was a spell of some kind. "A brave, loyal fool, but no less a fool. What talent she has comes from me, though it is very faint. I thought my mother's bloodline would end with me, until a woman who is what you would call a witch joined our travelling party. Back home, we would call her an enchantress. That's a powerful kind of witch, who can cast many types of spells, not just the one or two that she is best suited to."

Margareta nodded. Penelope would call her an enchantress, too, if she knew, though Margareta's power was limited by her nature. There had never been a mermaid witch before, and it was unlikely that there would be another. She could command water in ways that sent the other merfolk whispering and wishing she were far away, but any other spell – even the slightest blessing or curse – sapped her energy for hours. Penelope's power ran to…telepathy, she thought.

"Reading minds, yes," Penelope said. "Or strong emotions. I cannot change them, but I can perceive them. You should see Melitta's thoughts. Nothing but blurs of colour…and milk." She laughed.

Margareta ached to laugh with her, but she could not. Her father and her brothers depended on her silence. Yet with Penelope, she could perhaps hold something approaching a normal conversation. For the first time in Margareta's life, she wanted a friend. And a baby like Melitta, though motherhood would have to wait.

"I would like that," Penelope said. "Though I will ask one favour. Can you invite me into the garden every day? Arguing with the nuns here nearly wore me out before I made it outside." She winked. "I still might be in my room if I hadn't squeezed out a tear or two as I invoked Saint Godfrey, which is what they'll make of him if they are given their way. A brave, foolish man who would still be alive if he weren't such a brave fool. He should have left matters to the enchantress, as I did." Penelope smiled wanly. "I know you are curious. I will tell you the whole tale one day, but not today. I promise." She reached for the baby and Margareta reluctantly handed Melitta back to her mother.

Penelope's story could wait for another day.

Six

Erik trudged into his father's throne room with his eyes on the stone floor. He didn't want to meet his father's gaze at all, so when he approached the throne, he not only fell to his knees but bowed so low his forehead touched the stone.

"Father, I bring heavy news from Beacon Isle," he said.

The courtiers hushed each other, to better listen to his news.

"Crown Prince Philip is dead, as are all who

sailed with him," Erik continued.

"How did he die?" Father demanded.

"The ship we were on ran into a storm. Lightning struck the mast, which crushed the ship's cabin when it fell. All those within perished, and the ship sank." For the first time, Erik wished he'd been inside the cabin with his brother, for he knew what the king would ask next.

"How did you survive, when your brother perished?"

Erik wished he could bow lower, so that he sank right through the stones. "Philip sent me to fetch more wine, so I wasn't in the cabin. I was thrown into the ocean with everyone else, but by some miracle, I found my way to an undamaged boat, and made my way to shore." A mermaid, not a miracle, Erik was certain, but his father would never believe him. He barely believed himself, and he'd seen her with his own eyes.

"The sea is a perilous mistress, that no man can withstand. Not even a king. Poor Philip,"

Father said gravely.

No man, maybe. But the more Erik thought about it, the more he remembered about his time on that little boat. There'd been a girl, he remembered now. She'd hauled him aboard the boat, but somehow he'd ended up back in the water. That's when he saw the mermaid. Much later, he'd found himself back on board the boat with her, and he'd heard her ordering someone or something to take them home. The mermaids, or maybe even the ocean itself. And he'd arrived safely on the shore, but alone.

She couldn't have perished. It just wasn't possible. He'd return to Beacon Isle and find her and...

"Arise, Sir Erik. As crown prince, you are now heir to the throne in your brother's place," Father said, before the courtiers erupted in applause.

Crown prince? No, he had to return and find her. He'd dreamed of her every night, and every morning felt lost to find her gone.

"You will report back to me here on the morrow. Before you can become king, you have a lot to learn," Father continued.

Erik's heart sank. He resolved to learn all he could about kingship as fast as possible, the sooner to return to the mysterious girl. And he would find her. Some day, some how, he vowed, he would hold her in his arms again.

Seven

Unbeknownst to Margareta or Penelope, the nuns had commissioned a stone plaque to mark Sir Godfrey's grave. The stonemason brought it on his pony cart and the nuns decided to make it into a solemn celebration of the knight's deeds. Penelope and Melitta walked at the head of the procession, followed by most of the priory's residents, who had traded their white robes for mourning black. The pony cart brought up the rear, kicking up a great deal of dust that spurred Margareta to hurry to the front, where she could walk at Penelope's side, ostensibly to offer the widow support.

Penelope walked with her spine straight and her head held high. Her eyes were dry, and though her gown was as black as those worn by the nuns, her face was unshadowed.

Either there was little love between Sir Godfrey and Penelope, or her sorrow ran so deep she could not bear to show it on the surface, Margareta mused. She watched Penelope through the drawn-out erection ceremony, as the knight's monument was carried from the cart to its final resting place over his grave and a great number of prayers were uttered for his soul, but Margareta could not decide the truth of her friend's heart.

She had no chance to ask her during the sombre funeral feast in the priory's great hall, where the silence was broken by Melitta's insistent wail that it was time for her meal, too.

Penelope excused herself and Margareta followed her back to her chambers. The widow and her daughter slept in one of the priory's guest apartments, large, airy rooms with windows facing the sea. Penelope had set up her loom before one of the windows, where the light was brightest, though she had not yet started to make cloth.

Penelope took her accustomed position on the bed, propped up by pillows, as she fed Melitta. Margareta had seen the other woman feed the infant many times, but it still made her hungry for something she could not yet have. Not the milk — there were goats and cows aplenty on the island, and she could send down to the kitchens for fresh milk any time she wanted. No, she wanted a child like Melitta. To beget a child, she would need a husband, though, and would the child be enough to keep her from mourning if she lost her husband?

"You think me heartless, don't you?" Penelope said suddenly. She laughed softly. "No, I am not using magic to read your thoughts. I can see it in your eyes. You think because I do not cry for Godfrey, that I am not prostrate with grief at his passing, that I could not have loved him."

Margareta shook her head, but Penelope had turned her gaze on the baby at her breast.

"You're wrong, you know. He was a good, kind man, and I did love him. Perhaps not as much as he loved me, but then he was passionate in ways that I am not. And it killed him. He believed we were in danger, and he acted recklessly. Without thought. Anyone who'd paused for even a moment's reflection would have seen that the brigands were not interested in me. What was one waddling pregnant woman, when what they really wanted were the novices. Young maidens who were already prepared to serve. I've seen so many such women in the slave markets at home. Maidens fetch a higher price, though they do not remain maidens for long. Too many men believe dipping their wick in one can work miracles, and it's too late for the girls when the men discover what they were told is wrong. The brigands and slave sellers probably spread such rumours themselves, so that they can command a higher price for the girls they capture."

But there were no brigands on Beacon Isle, Margareta knew. Her father would have driven such ruffians off the island in a heartbeat, if he did not choose to hang them. She willed Penelope to read her mind and finally tell her what had happened the night her husband died.

Penelope looked up and her gaze met Margareta's. "I will tell you," she said slowly. "I know you think your rank protects you from the fate awaiting any common-born maiden the slavers capture, but you are wrong in that, too. Without a strong male protector or a powerful enchantress at your side, you are merely property in their eyes – and you can be bought and sold."

And on that chilling note, Penelope began her tale.

Eight

A rare summer storm had closed White Harbour to ships, for the normally calm stretch of water was battered by waves that would break stronger ships than the cog they rode in. The captain dropped anchor on the eastern side of the island, in what he called calm water, and sent them ashore in the boats.

Penelope and the other girls had clung to the sides of the boats as waves rocked them, threatening to capsize them. They were all soaked by the time they reached shore, where the novices huddled in a miserable little flock while one of the sailors headed for the nearest village to ask for a cart to carry the women.

Penelope settled on the sand to wait, for she felt the pains begin again. She didn't think they were birthing pains yet, but Godfrey worried so about her. The cart had been his idea, of course.

Then Kun, the enchantress, came ashore. She was as wet as the rest, for her strength lay in earth and not water magic, but she insisted she knew the island well, and the nearest village was further away than White Harbour, so they might as well walk.

Godfrey had the temerity to protest that Penelope could not walk so far in her condition, but something in her had rebelled at his coddling. She'd heaved herself to her feet, feeling an urge to move.

"But what if the cart comes and finds us gone?" Godfrey asked.

"Then it can come and get us," Kun said with a shrug. The afternoon sun shone, but her dark hair seemed to drink the light instead of reflecting it. Even Godfrey would not look at her for long before turning away.

Kun beckoned for the novices to follow her, and they made a strange procession. Penelope leaned on Godfrey's arm, for the knight's horse had remained aboard the ship and he walked with the rest of them.

They walked through the fields in the afternoon light, so the setting sun was in their eyes when they entered the wood. Penelope welcomed the cool darkness, but there were more than trees waiting for them. She heard the shouts, but couldn't see past the novices in front of her. She and Godfrey had fallen to the rear, so when one of the brigands circled around to attack them from behind, Godfrey wrenched his sword from its scabbard and charged the man.

More men stepped out of the trees to assist Godfrey's man, and for a moment, he was surrounded before they cut him down. It was done so quickly, so silently that he was dead before she was aware of what had happened.

Penelope felt magic billowing out from the enchantress, and she bit her lip to offer what little help she could. Then she saw into the men's minds. They wanted the girls, but more than that, they wanted to chase them as they ran, their desire building as they hunted. Penelope herself was dismissed as poor sport, but when one of the novices bolted, their fierce joy was almost unbearable as they leaped as one to follow her. Penelope fell to her knees.

Kun's magic engulfed them all, shaking the earth so hard no one remained standing but the enchantress herself.

One of the men fell near Penelope, and she was surprised to see he wore fine clothes. They all did. Brigandry evidently paid well on Beacon Isle.

Kun shouted something and the man before her began to shimmer, then shrink. He gave a horrible cry, but he grew smaller and smaller until Penelope could have cupped him in her hands. Then he shivered, throwing his cloak out wide and it caught the wind, buoying him up like wings. No, they were wings.

Penelope watched in amazement as the brigands turned into birds, which flew away.

Then pain engulfed her once more, and she knew that this pain was not the same as before. Her baby was coming, and she was helpless to stop her birthing blood from mingling with her husband's lifeblood on the road.

Nine

"I will not do this!" Margareta burst out. After being silent so long, her voice sounded strange in her ears. "I will not save them from a fate they so richly deserve. She should have killed them, not let them fly away. How dare they…"

Penelope's mouth dropped open in shock. "But an enchantress cannot use her power to kill. It is against the laws of their kind. If she does, she will be enslaved like the other djinn, who were once free to practice magic until they turned to evil."

Margareta would not be silenced. "So an enchantress who puts down a pack of rabid dogs who prey on women is punished, while the men get off lightly, with the gift of flight?"

"That was the enchantress's choice of punishment. I am sure Mistress Kun had her reasons. A lesser witch does not question an enchantress, for she understands far more than I ever will," Penelope faltered.

"Where is this enchantress now?" Margareta demanded.

"I do not know. I was busy with childbirth when she left and I did not see her again," Penelope replied.

So she could not question the enchantress, Margareta mused. But there was one person she could speak to, who would not be allowed to hold back information this time.

She stormed through the house to her father's solar. He had aged since she'd seen him last, though it had only been a few weeks. Right now, though, she didn't care if he looked twice his age.

"I won't do it. I won't stay silent. They deserve their fate," she said through gritted teeth.

"They're boys. Your brothers. Boys shouldn't be punished for pulling a prank. They weren't hurting anybody. Those novices were too easily frightened." Father dismissed her concerns with a wave of his hand.

"And what of the witch? Or Lady Penelope? Or Sir Godfrey, the knight they murdered?" Margareta demanded. "A man is dead. His wife a widow, his child fatherless. They demand justice."

Her father surveyed the study. "Yet I don't see them here. Just you."

Margareta slammed her fist into the table. "Yes, me. The daughter you duped into helping you free my dastardly brothers from a curse they deserve."

"They killed a man who attacked them, Meg. There is no crime in that. They are my sons, and one day Beacon Isle will belong to them. In the meantime, they carry my justice from one end of the island to the other. Perhaps they might have overpowered the man, and brought him here to face justice instead of killing him outright, but there were a lot of women present who might have been in danger from the madman. If they were here, I could ask them, but they are not, and they will not return until the curse is broken. A curse you swore you would break."

"That was before I knew how much they deserved it!" Margareta cried. "If I break this curse, one day they will be masters of Beacon Isle, and heaven help the islanders when you are gone. There will be no justice, for they will be lords who take whatever they will, and no woman will be safe. I will not be a part of this, Father."

"So you will let your brothers remain birds forever, because you, a girl who has not been taught to rule like her brothers have from their infancy, think you know better?"

Margareta folded her arms across her chest. "Any village idiot knows better that to torment innocent women for their own amusement. I would do a far better job at ruling this island than any of my brothers."

"No woman can rule," Father scoffed. "That is why girls must marry. So their husband can rule their lands with the strength required to hold them, or they would soon lose them to conquest."

In the human world, Margareta knew this to be true, but beneath the waves, it was a different story. "Not my kind. Under the surface, women rule the oceans. And the men who think they are strong enough to challenge us for our domain die," she said fiercely.

The Master of Beacon Isle leaned back in his chair, considering her. "Very well. If you lift the curse on my sons, I will give you Beacon Isle as your dowry when you marry."

Margareta held his gaze, knowing the lie that lurked beneath his promise. Her kind did not marry, and no human male would survive long in her bed. But he would only need to survive long enough to claim her dowry, and Beacon

Isle would be safe. Her brothers could never inherit.

"We have an accord," she said.

The Master was quick to follow up on what he thought was his advantage. "Indeed we do. See that you keep your promise and save my sons."

Mutely, Margareta nodded. If by breaking the curse, she could free Beacon Isle from the curse of her brothers, her silence was a small price to pay. One which would yield lands, a husband and maybe even the one thing she wanted most – a child like Melitta.

Ten

Later that evening, in the solitude of her chambers, Margareta took a knife and sliced the skin of her arm, letting the blood flow. She was a weak spellcaster with anything that wasn't water, and she wanted this spell to work. What might take another enchantress merely a drop of blood took much more from Margareta.

She wove her magic carefully, making sure the spell affected only herself. When she was done, silence settled over her tongue. There would be no mistakes or changes of heart this time. She would not, nay, could not speak until her brothers' curse broke and they returned to Beacon Isle. Until then, her voice would not be heard.

Not a word or a laugh or a single sound would pass her lips for more than six years, when fate intervened.

For a siren whose voice is never heard is hardly a siren at all. Maybe enough to make a man wonder whether she might make a suitable wife.

Eleven

Had Beacon Isle been this green the last time he was here? Erik wondered as the island came into view. He couldn't remember. Last time, he'd been too caught up in the sheer adventure of it all, his first sea voyage, his first journey at all. He'd had responsibilities then, too, which had taken much of his time. Armour did not polish itself and salt from the sea voyage had conspired to make his duties tenfold more difficult.

He'd learned a lot about the sea since then,

and those who made their living on it. Enough to know how to keep his sword from rusting, and to wear leather armour, when he wore any at all. He was on a mission of peace, not war, and he was under strict instructions not to risk his life unnecessarily.

Just as his brother, Philip, had not risked his own in anything more ordinary than a sea voyage. A voyage that had both blessed and cursed Erik, for he alone had survived. He and a girl he swore he'd find.

Six years it had taken to convince his father to allow him to go to sea. Anything could have happened to her in that time. She might have died, or married, or run far away from Beacon Isle, but that was the last place he'd seen her, so that was where he would start his search.

That Beacon Isle was at the heart of other, stranger stories than his intrigued him. His father dismissed the tales as the fantasies of sailors embellished by nurses who wished to frighten children. Yet Erik knew something his father did not – he had his own dreams and memories to go on, the proof of his own eyes. A moment of foggy memory that would not leave him alone gave credence to all the tales the way nothing else could.

And yet…

Erik sighed. The tales told so many conflicting things, it was hard to make any sense of them. That was why we sought the source of such tales — and the library on Beacon Isle was famed far and wide. Why, it was said that some of the books from the library of the ancients, which burned a thousand years ago, had been salvaged and were kept even now in the priory at Beacon Isle. Not that he wanted scrolls from so far afield. He wanted the history of Beacon Isle itself and the waters surrounding it. Especially the waters…

Water he would have to cross if he was to find what he sought, Erik told himself, forcing himself to step across the gangplank to shore. There, that was not so difficult, he chided himself as his boots touched the cobbled surface of the dock.

He'd surprised himself with how easy it was. Weren't all seas the same water, after all? He'd sailed many of them in his thankless quest, but still he had no more answers than when he'd started. That's why Beacon Isle must hold the answers. Here his quest had begun, and here it would end, one way or the other. Either he would find the answers he sought, or he would be forced to agree with his father that whatever he'd seen in the water was nothing but an illusion invented by his own fevered brain.

Erik took a coin, tossed it into the air and caught it on the back of his hand. Heads and he was delusional; tails and he would find what he sought here. Erik lifted his hand, and cheered aloud when he did not see his father's engraved profile on the uppermost side of the coin. He would find something here, he was certain of it. If not her, then perhaps the book he wanted waited in the library.

Erik itched to begin his search, but he knew

better. Politics demanded he present himself to the Master of Beacon Isle first, for he was his father's son, and his father had his own reasons for keeping the Master happy.

Aside from its value to Erik, Beacon Isle was one of the richest trading ports in the region, accepting goods from all corners of the globe and trading them far and wide. It was strategic to the defence of half a dozen countries that surrounded it, and it had its own navy that served Beacon Isle and acknowledged no king as its sovereign except the Master of Beacon Isle.

A Master, yet not a king. It even piqued Erik's curiosity how a man could hold such power without a crown. Almost as though there was more to Beacon Isle than anyone thought.

Calling his thanks to the captain for the ride, Erik set out across Harbour Town to reach the Master's house, and the priory beyond.

The town quickly dropped behind him as he ascended the hill where legend said one of the saints had founded the first priory on the site. The rude wooden huts that had once stood there were long gone, replaced by the edifice of white and grey stone that occupied the crown of the hill overlooking White Harbour. On a beautiful day such as this, it was a view fit for a king.

Erik stepped through the gate into the bailey, his rich clothing announcing his arrival before he could open his mouth.

Men set off for the port to bring his belongings while another asked for his name and ushered him into the great hall, where he was offered food and wine while he waited for the Master.

Bemused, Erik accepted the offer of wine, wondering how far afield the vintage had come from, for it was surely too cold for grapes on Beacon Isle. A cautious sip told him all he needed to know – the wine was not from grapes at all, but made with berries in the style made famous by a kingdom to the south of his father's that backed onto the mountains, and a particular favourite at his father's court. His father had hinted that a marriage between Erik and the king's only daughter would be advantageous for both kingdoms, but Erik had no intention of marrying a woman he'd never met. Life would include enough unhappiness without sharing it with a woman he didn't love.

"Prince Erik. It is an honour," a deep voice said. The man who entered the hall looked ancient, instead of the same age as Erik's own father. But no one else would walk into the great hall of Beacon Isle like a king granting a great favour to one of his subjects. This ageing nobleman was stronger than he appeared, for no weakling could hold the rich lands of Beacon Isle without even a crown to legitimise his claim to the neighbouring kingdoms.

Erik set his goblet on the table, turned and bowed. "Master Nicholas. I thought you would send one of your sons to greet me. I had no idea that you would take the time to meet me yourself. The honour is mine."

Master Nicholas's eyes clouded with

something like grief. "My sons, like so many others, have gone on a long journey to seek redemption for their sins. I hope to see them home soon, but I fear I shall find them changed men, after such a long absence. Many years."

Erik murmured something appropriate about how proud he must be of his sons. While Master Nicholas waxed lyrical about his numerous sons and their even more numerous talents, Erik wondered what it would be like to undertake a crusade to free the Holy Land like Nicholas' sons evidently had. It seemed such a pointless business that one would surely have had to commit some truly grievous sins in order to require such lengthy reparation.

He debated whether Master Nicholas's boys had done something particularly bad, or whether the fervour of others had caught them up like so many other young noblemen. Surely the latter.

"And what brings you here to my humble isle?" Master Nicholas asked.

Erik managed a smile. "Why, a quest of my own. I have developed a singular interest in the history of the region, and I've found a large gap in the history of Beacon Isle. Considering the fame of your library, I naturally assumed the information I sought would be here."

Master Nicholas laughed, though it sounded hollow. He knew as well as Erik that the one thing Erik's father, and in fact all the neighbouring kings, wanted to know, was which king had last held sovereignty over Beacon Isle…and how, if at all, he had lost it. Such a secret would surely be within the archives here on Beacon Isle.

"I will see to it that you have a research assistant who is an expert in all of our library collections, the day after tomorrow. First, you must rest from your journey, and tomorrow is our harvest feast, so you must join us. I will introduce you to my daughter at the feast, too."

Erik suppressed a sigh. What was it with men once they had a daughter? The moment she was old enough, they all wanted to marry the poor girl off, and they all looked eagerly at him as the prospective husband. As if a good marriage began with a desire to please the girl's father, and not the girl herself. When he found the girl he wanted, he would do everything within his power to please the girl. She was the one he intended to share his life with, after all.

He made noises that he hoped sounded eager, then escaped the Master as quickly as he could without being rude.

<h1 style="text-align:center">Twelve</h1>

Penelope finished tying the laces of Margareta's gown. "There," she breathed, standing back to admire her handiwork.

"She looks beautiful, Mama. Like a princess," six-year-old Melitta squealed, clapping her hands. "Can I be Harvest Queen, too, when I'm all grown up?"

"She's not the Harvest Queen, sweetheart," Penelope said. "The Harvest Queen wears gold, not blue. Lady Margareta is the Lady of Beacon Isle, and one day she'll be the Mistress of the whole island."

"What about me?" the child demanded.

Margareta couldn't hide her smile. When she was that age, she'd admired the village girls chosen to be Harvest Queens, and wished that some day she might be one of them. Now, she knew better. The girl chosen to lord it over her fellows at each Harvest Festival never lacked for partners when the dancing started, and she never failed to find a husband before the first winter snows. From the moment the blessed crown of flowers touched the Queen's head, she became the sole focus of every man present. For the blessing was one of fertility…and any man who could win the Queen's affections that night was certain to sire a child on her, hence the rapid weddings.

She remembered her brothers being among previous queens' suitors. As a child, she'd seen the uncrowned queens marrying other men, and she'd pitied her brothers for being rejected. Now, she realised that wasn't the case — the girls had been hurriedly married off to save what honour they had left after her brothers had finished with them.

That wouldn't be the fate of tonight's Queen, however – Margareta was certain of that. Queen Gerda was safe from her cursed brothers, and well known to be walking out with young Kay, a boy orphaned by the very same shipwreck that Prince Philip and his entourage had died in. Margareta hoped she'd see Gerda and Kay reach a marriage accord tonight, and that the competition of other men wanting her hand would spur the boy into action before he lost the girl.

"Perhaps when you are older, you will be Harvest Queen, and I shall make you a beautiful dress in gold," Penelope said to her daughter.

"No! Blue like Lady Margareta!" the child shrieked.

Penelope shook her head. "Your spirit is all spit and fire, child. If you are ever Harvest Queen, the boys will burn the city for you, thinking it is Midsummer and not harvest at all." She dropped her voice lower so only Margareta could hear. "I already told you, the competition will frighten the boy off. I'll wager you the first piece of velvet off my loom that he is too cowardly to ask the girl. He doesn't think he's worthy of her."

Margareta had to admit Penelope had an edge on her, being able to read the boy's thoughts and all, but Margareta wanted to believe some happiness would come of tonight's feast. Besides, watching the Harvest Queen while she was stuck at the high table, where no man would dare ask her to dance, would provide some amusement in an otherwise tedious evening.

"Let us go," Penelope said, straightening the veil she wore over her hair. To the two veiled novices who'd appeared in the doorway, she added, "Make sure she's in bed as soon as she's finished her supper. I don't want her sneaking downstairs to the feast again."

The novices murmured their agreement.

To the sound of Melitta screaming about

wanting to come to the ball, too, Penelope and Margareta made their way down to the great hall. Penelope's dove grey gown and matching veil marked her as a widow, though she was long since finished with her mourning period. Margareta's blue gown glowed like the sky above, setting off her curved figure to perfection. When she arrived at the door to the great hall, silence fell without anyone needing to announce her name. The breath caught in every male throat as each and every man present desired to possess her, and every feminine gasp spoke volumes about how much they wished they could be her.

Margareta did not need the Harvest Queen's crown or Penelope's mind-reading magic to know these things – it was plain in the expression on every face. Even when her tongue was silent, a siren's body sang a song so enticing no human could resist.

Ignoring all the eyes on her, Margareta led the way to the high table. She paid little heed to the men already seated at her father's right and left hands as she headed for her accustomed seat at the far end of the table. She shared her small bench with Penelope, because after her, Penelope was the second highest ranking woman in the room.

The feast itself passed much like any other — everyone ate too much and drank more, until the volume of their collective voices rose to a roar that echoed around the room. When the roar approached what Margareta thought was its crescendo, her father rose to announce the Harvest Queen, who would open the dancing.

Clad in the traditional saffron-coloured gown worn by Harvest Queens for as long as Margareta could remember, Gerda approached the dais and dropped a deep curtsey, letting her skirt puddle around her as she'd no doubt practised. Father, as Master of Beacon Isle, laid the blessed crown of flowers on the girl's head and bade her to rise as royalty.

The moment the crown touched her hair, the atmosphere in the room changed from the sated merriment after a feast to charged anticipation.

"We're not the only ones betting on who the little queen chooses to be her king," Penelope whispered.

If it weren't for her spell of silence, Margareta would have had to smother a laugh. A lot of young men had turned their eyes on Gerda, as though seeing the girl for the first time. Poor Kay, who'd sat beside her at the feast, now stared into his mug of ale as though he couldn't bear to see how beautiful Gerda looked tonight.

The Master gave the order and the tables and benches were swept aside to make space for the highlight of the evening – the Harvest Ball.

Gerda and her golden gown were soon hidden among a crowd of eager young men, while other couples lined up for a country dance. Margareta longed to be among them, but her father would never allow her to dance, because there was no knowing when her siren side might take over and decide the poor boy needed to die instead of dance with her.

So Margareta watched and kept Penelope company, for no man would think of asking the widow of a saint to do something as frivolous as dancing, or so Penelope said.

"How fares young Kay?" Penelope asked.

Margareta pointed at the boy, who sat moodily in the corner with his ale.

Penelope clapped her hands. "You'll be taking me out on the boat for sure. I hope we'll have fine weather tomorrow, because I fancy a trip out on the ocean!"

So would Margareta, she admitted to herself. To be out on the waves, breathing in the salt spray and listening to the swish of the hull cutting smoothly through the sea, instead of the smoky air in the hall full of music and shouting and the stomp of booted feet.

"Lady, would you do me the honour of joining me in this dance?" the man to Margareta's right asked, extending his hand.

Margareta shook her head and Penelope piped up, "The Lady Margareta is under a vow of silence until her brothers return."

"But that won't stop you dancing, will it, my lady?" the man persisted. "Your father said –"

"Her father wants his sons to return just as much as Lady Margareta," Penelope said smoothly, cutting the man off.

Margareta dared to look into his eyes. They lit up with his eager grin, as if he truly didn't believe she could refuse him. She lowered her gaze, frowned, then shook her head emphatically.

"Meg, be a good girl. Go dance with the king's envoy," the Master ordered, stabbing a finger at the dance floor.

She shot her father a look of surprise. Didn't he care what happened to the ambassador? What if something happened and her true nature took over and…

"Dance, girl!" the Master commanded.

Unable to refuse, Margareta laid her hand on the envoy's proffered arm, and allowed herself to be led onto the dance floor. She shot Penelope an imploring look, begging her friend to keep an eye on her thoughts and that of the ambassador.

Margareta glimpsed Penelope's grave nod before she and the ambassador were whirled away into the organised chaos that was a country dance.

Thirteen

The moment she stepped into the great hall, Erik knew his search was over before it had even started. She was here – the girl in his dreams. Or at least he thought she was.

He didn't remember her having curves like that, or perhaps he'd been too young to notice. Her dark hair was hidden mostly under a veil, but a rebellious tendril had escaped. She moved like a stately lady, which indeed she was, if she was the Master's daughter. The grey-clad widow at her side looked like her companion or her chaperone, Erik wasn't sure.

The girl sat beside him, close enough to reach out and touch, though he didn't dare. She shared a bench with her chaperone, he judged, when the widow shot him a shrewd glance that seemed to size up his very soul.

He met the widow's gaze, willing her to believe that his intentions toward the girl were honourable. How could they not be? He'd come here to find her, and here she was, not a foot from him!

Erik scarcely tasted a bite of his meal as he struggled to keep his breathing even. He wanted to blurt out everything to her, everything that had kept him away for the last six years and what brought him here now, but every time he tried to say something to her, his voice died in his throat. What did a man say to the woman of his dreams, when he saw her for the first time in six years?

And so he waited for her to break the silence. A silence he should not have noticed, amid the noise of a hall full of people making merry to celebrate the harvest, and yet the silence stretched in his mind until it lay like a great gulf between them.

The tables were cleared away to make space for dancing, and Erik's heart leaped. A ball! At home in his father's court, the ladies would form up and dance, spinning around one another like flower petals blown by the wind, before coming together as the complex pattern drew them in at the end of the dance.

Erik held his breath for a moment in eager anticipation as the first girls stepped out into the cleared space. But they were followed soon after by men, forming up in couples like no ball Erik had ever been to. Only then did it strike him that none of those present were nobles – the hall was full of common people, dressed in such bright colours that it hadn't occurred to him to look more closely at their clothes. This was a prosperous place indeed if even the peasants' clothes were as coloured as those of his father's courtiers.

He waited for the girl beside him to join the

dance, but she remained resolutely in her seat. No partner, perhaps?

Before he'd truly thought the words through, he blurted out a clumsy invitation for her to dance with him.

Her eyes met his – two blue jewels that seemed to hold the depths of the ocean inside them. But the one thing that they didn't hold was any spark of recognition. She shook her head, which made the grey widow pipe up in the girl's support.

Erik's heart ached at the thought that this wasn't the girl he was looking for – how could she not recognise him, when he knew her instantly? – but his ever-optimistic imagination ventured that if she had changed in the intervening time, so had he, and it would take time for her to remember him. Just because he hadn't been able to forget the shipwreck and how she'd saved him from it, didn't mean she had been similarly affected. Perhaps she had endured many shipwrecks, and rescued many helpless boys, and there was nothing special about him at all.

No, he'd felt it then and he knew it now. There was something between them, a connection that once made could not be broken. He felt it in his bones.

The grey widow would not stop him from dancing with her.

Erik countered her arguments as to why the girl shouldn't dance, and just as he felt he had the upper hand, a male voice cut in.

Master Nicholas ordered the girl to dance with him.

The girl's eyes widened, and she looked affronted at her father. She was no dutiful daughter, this one. If not for her vow of silence, the girl would have given her father a piece of her undoubtedly strong mind.

The Master either ignored or dismissed her rebellious glance, and repeated his command.

With an expression that said her father would rue this later, the girl rose gracefully, every inch a veritable queen as she took Erik's hastily proffered arm.

The dancers parted and bowed to allow them to take their place at the head of the formation. The musicians faltered, then began anew, hesitantly at first, then more boldly as the girl stepped across the divide to place her palm against Erik's.

Heat flared between his hand and hers, surprising him. She should have been cold, icy, not warm to the touch. Perhaps he was wrong, and she wasn't…

Deep blue eyes sucked at his soul as they whirled among the other dancers, assessing him as frankly as though she were the Master himself.

Erik stumbled, forgetting the steps, nearly sending them crashing into another couple.

Her arms grew rigid around him, steering him bodily away from the others for all the world as though she had the strength to lift him off his feet. Or pluck him from the ocean into a boat.

Now it was Erik's turn to stare at her. Either she was, or she wasn't.

They moved apart, as required by the steps of the dance, and Erik was forced to partner three other girls before he could approach her again.

"Do you remember me?" he asked urgently. "That day in the water?"

She grimaced as he trod on her foot.

Erik opened his mouth to apologise, but she brought her slippered heel down so hard on his instep all that came out was a pained yelp.

She broke free of his hold, weaving expertly through the dancers until she reached the edge of the room. An imperious wave of her hand brought a servant with a goblet. The girl took the goblet, turned on her bone-breaking heel, and strode out of the great hall, with the grey widow hard on her heels.

Disappointment welled up in Erik's throat. If he hadn't been so clumsy, she might have answered his question. Then he'd know if she truly was the right one.

With considerably less grace than the girl, Erik made his way through the dancers and back to the dais, where he slumped to the bench beside Master Nicholas's chair.

Gesturing for a servant to fill his cup with wine, Erik said to Master Nicholas, "Your daughter is certainly a very spirited girl."

Master Nicholas drained his cup. "That she is. Break her, and she's yours. Consider her a gift."

Erik's mouth dropped open, and he hastened to close it. Break her? She would outlast the strongest granite, Erik was certain. For a wave might break against a rock, but no man could master the ocean. Least of all him.

"My father would welcome a marriage alliance between his kingdom and yours," Erik managed to say. He bowed to the Master and bade him a good night before heading up to his chambers.

It wasn't until he was alone in bed that Erik realised he hadn't even asked for her name.

Fourteen

The moment the door to the great hall closed behind Penelope, Margareta slowed her steps. Her feet hurt after being stomped on by that boor. What had possessed him to ask her to dance when he was so abysmal at dancing, and he didn't even know the steps?

The water in the ewer splashed over the side with the force of the waves Margareta's fury had created. She forced herself to calm down, at least a little.

"From the moment he entered the room, he

fell under your spell," Penelope said softly. "He could think of no one and nothing else but you."

That made him no different to any other man present tonight, Margareta knew. The lure of a siren was almost impossible to resist, which was why she'd refused to dance with him. What had her father been thinking, telling her to dance with him? If she killed some king's ambassador, there could be war. Already she seethed at his touch.

"I didn't read your father's thoughts, so I don't know the answer to that," Penelope replied. "I was too busy keeping an eye on you and your lover boy."

She would never take that boor as her lover, Margareta fumed. His thoughts had undoubtedly been filled with all the things he dreamed of doing to her if he could get her alone and naked. Margareta's money was on him being the forceful sort, who dreamed of pinning her to a bed beneath his weight and forcing himself between her legs. Marginally better than the ones who delighted in the dream of forcing her to her knees to pleasure him with her mouth.

"Neither of those," Penelope said cheerfully. "His thoughts were quite refreshing, really. Yes, they were of you, but mostly he focussed on your face. And the light was sort of blue, like you were under water. There's something different about him. Not that it really matters. You probably won't see him again. He's here on some sort of quest, but he keeps those thoughts hidden. At least, he did last night, when you were there to distract him." Penelope dropped her voice to a conspiratorial whisper. "Judging by the tone of his thoughts, he'd make a more attentive lover than most men. He was genuinely sorry when he stepped on your feet."

Not as sorry as Margareta intended to make him if he ever touched her feet again, she resolved grimly.

Penelope laughed. "I'm sure you'll think of some truly diabolical torture for the man. You can tell me what you've decided in the morning. I am going to return to my chambers, where I hope the sisters have managed to get Melitta to sleep, and where I intend to do the same."

Margareta wished her friend a silent good night. When she was certain Penelope was far enough away, Margareta left her room and headed for the beach. A swim in the cool water would do her good. She could dive down deep and change the currents to her heart's content until she felt better. Damn her father for putting her too close to that man. It was almost as though he wanted her to kill the ambassador.

No, surely not.

Fifteen

By the following morning, Margareta was back to her usual sunny self as she sat in the brightly lit bower with Penelope. As had become their custom, Penelope worked on her weaving, while Margareta busied herself copying some of the older, crumbling manuscripts from the library before they became entirely unreadable.

Father often commented that writing was a man's job, and not suitable for a lady. The priory had a group of monks whose sole occupation was to illuminate the manuscripts they found in the library, as Margareta knew well, but she'd watched the monks at their work, and it left a lot to be desired. Oh, their books were beautiful enough, written in lovely letters and illustrated with the most exquisite pictures, but for every manuscript they copied, another dozen crumbled to dust, they were so slow. Completing a single page could take days, the way the monks did it, and on her father's death, this library, like all of Beacon Isle, would be hers. And she did not want to lose any of the texts it contained.

So, while the monks made beautiful books, she collected the scrolls they left behind, and transcribed what she could decipher. Her pages were plain but readable, which was more than she could say about the originals, and if the monks wanted to turn her work into beautiful books, at least they'd still have the text from the source to go by, instead of it being lost altogether.

One winter, when the harbour had completely iced over and kept all the ships away for weeks, Margareta had run out of ink. Bored beyond belief, she'd undertaken to reorganise the library. Through the centuries, the books and scrolls had been placed on shelves based on the date they were bought or last read. That meant the earliest scrolls had crumbled together into indecipherable fragments that Margareta lacked the patience to piece together, but it also appeared that some of the older scrolls had been removed from their original shelves and shoved back into pigeonholes which were already occupied by more recent manuscripts, making a mess that had only worsened through the centuries.

Two days after she'd finished her Herculean task, the harbour ice had finally cracked and more ink had arrived.

Margareta had intended to write a document, summarising her filing system so that anyone could easily find what they sought, but in the course of her cleaning, she'd found so many scrolls in need of copying before their contents disappeared altogether that she'd had other priorities for her time. Even now, she fought against time to preserve all of them.

Most days, she was fascinated by what she read. Stories about wars fought in lands she'd never heard of, with exotic names and all sorts of strange animals, or accounts of men and events she couldn't even begin to understand. Senates and votes and pharaohs and all manner of strange words came up in these manuscripts.

Today's scroll tried her patience. Not only had the writer failed to put spaces between the Latin words so that the reader might know where one word ended and the next began, but the words themselves left a foul taste in her mouth. The unknown writer who had first penned the words believed that all the ills of the world could be cured if only husbands controlled their wives, who were apparently all violent, uncontrollable creatures. So either they could be controlled, or they couldn't, Margareta fumed. She was tempted to drop this scroll in the fire and be done with it. A violent, uncontrollable creature…why, she hadn't attacked anyone yet!

The servant who entered the room was a welcome interruption.

"Mistress, the Master asks for some scrolls from the library, which he says only you can find."

Margareta glanced at Penelope.

Penelope waved her away. "Go, help your father. I'm poor company anyway. One moment, I am so close to getting this cloth right, and the next…it falls apart and I must try again. If I hadn't seen that finished piece of velvet with my own eyes, I'd swear it wasn't possible. Perhaps I should stick to silk."

Margareta smiled. She knew Penelope would never give up. The woman was as gifted with a needle as she was with a loom, and if anyone could create a new cloth by herself, it was Penelope.

"Bring back something interesting this time, instead of that dry old history scroll. Knights and dragons and…violent, uncontrollable creatures," Penelope called after Margareta.

Margareta chuckled silently to herself. These six years of silence would have been impossible but for Penelope's mind-reading talents. As she marched purposefully through the corridors of her father's house and into the priory, Margareta resolved to deal with this errand as quickly as possible, because she knew exactly which book to bring back to share with Penelope.

Sixteen

A servant brought Erik breakfast, along with the welcome message that Master Nicholas had not only granted his request to use the library today, but he'd given him an assistant to help him navigate their collection of books. Erik was under no illusions that the assistant wouldn't report his every move back to the Master, but it was of little concern. He could easily hide his father's mission under the cover of his own project. Master Nicholas would think him crazy, which he undoubtedly was, and leave him to his own devices.

Erik wolfed down his breakfast, dressed and demanded to be shown the way to the famous library. The maidservant lost no time in leading the way – Erik had trouble keeping up with the girl as she trotted through the richly decorated passageways. It wasn't until they reached the bare corridor that marked the start of the priory that she slowed down. Erik thought he heard her breathe a sigh of relief as she weaved through the monks. Almost as though she feared walking through the corridors of the house proper. Or was he the one who scared her?

The girl abruptly stopped, then spun on her heel to stand beside the doorway instead of passing through it. She dropped a deep curtsey. "The library, sir." She dashed off before he could thank her.

Erik stared after her for a moment before giving himself a shake. He had his own mystery to solve – he didn't need to know what frightened the maids of Beacon Isle.

He stepped through the doorway and had to stop. He'd entered what might have been just another passage, if it weren't lined from floor to ceiling with shelves full of books. Erik couldn't suppress a grin. This was what he was here for.

Selecting a leather spine at random, he pulled a book from the shelf. The pages were filled with strange symbols, interspersed with letters he recognised. Erik laughed. Trust Beacon Isle to keep their books in some sort of code, indecipherable to all but those who lived here. Maybe an assistant would be useful after all.

An assistant who didn't appear to be anywhere in the library. Erik strolled between the shelves, not sure where to start. When he reached the end of the corridor, he realised he'd been mistaken – the biggest library he'd ever seen was merely the antechamber to the real, much more massive collection that filled a chamber easily as big as the great hall itself. Some shelves were divided into pigeonholes occupied by scrolls instead of birds, while others were nigh as tall as him to accommodate huge books that would take two men to lift.

A table sat in the middle of the room, as large as one of the feasting tables in the hall below, dwarfing the stack of books that lay at its head.

"Uh, hello?" Erik called.

From behind the stack of books, which were taller than he'd thought, a figure rose to her feet.

Erik's heart leaped as he recognised the lady he'd danced with last night. The Master's daughter, whose name he still did not know.

"Beg pardon, my lady, but your father told me to meet my assistant here, as I'll be doing some research about the island's history in your remarkable library. Can you tell me where he might be?" Erik ventured.

The girl's eyes grew flinty. She picked up the hefty stack of books, thrust them at his chest so hard she nearly knocked him over, then stalked out of the library without a word.

Erik set the books down on the table, wondering how such a slight girl had had the strength lift such a heavy load.

There was still no sign of the promised assistant, so he sat down and flicked open the first book.

He found a list of ships, along with their date of arrival, cargo, and duty paid on that cargo. They dated from the previous century.

A quick examination of the other books in the pile revealed they all contained information about the history of the isle.

Had the Master given him his own daughter to be a research assistant? No wonder the lady was angry at being assigned a task that surely should have been given to a servant.

"Thank you," Erik called after her, but he doubted she heard. Even if she did, she certainly didn't return, so Erik set to work.

Seventeen

This could only end badly. A polite ambassador who did his best to charm her spelled trouble for her and for himself, Margareta knew. Her father couldn't possibly have meant for her to work closely with him as his assistant. Why, the ambassador wouldn't last the week. She'd already seen that look in his eyes that told her he was under her spell, and not only was he less boorish away from the dance floor, but she could feel her heart softening toward him. If she hardened her heart to him like any other man, he might stand a chance. But if she let him win her over, maybe even try to seduce her a little, the ambassador was a dead man, and whatever king he served would want to know why.

And whatever he thought about the matter, Margareta knew that her father was no longer capable of leading the island to war, let alone victory.

Margareta didn't often question her father any more, and not just because she maintained her vow of silence. She'd seen him deteriorate from the strong man she remembered, revered and feared as a child, to a shadow of himself. Oh, some days, like at the Harvest Festival, he covered his thinning hair with a horsehair wig and dressed to outshine even the richest merchants. But others…Margareta sighed.

Her father had taken to his bed today, much the worse for last night's wine, and he refused to see anyone. Margareta was the exception, for no one could keep her out. Not even her father on days like this.

The moment he saw her, he sat up, leaving his bedcap on the pillow. "Have they returned? Do you bring word?" he asked eagerly.

Margareta shook her head. No, her brothers had not returned. She hadn't yet broken the curse.

His face crumpled. Some days he dissolved into tears, but today wasn't one of them. Instead, his face twisted into a snarl. "Bring them back. You must bring them back. Without my sons, the isle will be defenceless against all those kings who fancy my island. Not least of all that sneaky ambassador who's rooting around for his king. He'll never get what he's looking for. See that you help him with the books, for the sooner he's off the island, the better. You'll take care of him, won't you?"

Margareta's heart sank. When her father was having a bad day like this one, she could refuse him nothing. So she nodded dutifully, praying that the ambassador would leave before he came to harm.

Eighteen

Every day for a week, Margareta set a stack of books on the table for the ambassador, then left him to his reading. After the way he'd looked and spoken to her that first day, she didn't dare to spend more than a few minutes in his company. If she lingered, he would give in to the desires she could read clearly through his eyes, and when he did, he would die.

Much safer to let him read the port logs than to meet his gaze and wonder what it would feel like to surrender to her siren desires. Her father made them sound like such terrible things, but anything you didn't want to stop doing surely resulted in a great deal of pleasure. How could that be so terrible?

Yet every time the ambassador bade her good morning, thanking her for the books and wishing her a pleasant day, she longed to linger. The only thing that stopped her was the stack of ledgers she'd handed to him, and the sheer boredom she'd experienced on the rare occasions she'd copied one out.

Why anyone wanted to know which ships had touched at the island a hundred years ago, she wasn't sure, but she had no intention of keeping him company while he read books that would put any normal man to sleep.

Yet he certainly didn't sleep, as evident by the pages of notes he scrawled each day. Margareta had glanced at them, but his writing was harder to read than the books she copied. What she could decipher appeared to be records of ships lost near the island. The list looked long after three days, and grew with each new day.

It seemed to Margareta that merchants would avoid what appeared to be such a dangerous trading port, but a quick peek at the harbour outside told her otherwise. Only on the rare winters when the ocean froze over entirely was White Harbour ever empty. It was almost full today.

The ambassador didn't seem to notice, though. He was too intent on reading the books she'd given him yesterday.

Margareta thumped a new stack onto the table beside him and turned to leave.

To linger was to lose control, which she couldn't do, Margareta reminded herself.

He caught her arm, and though she tried to pull away, his grip on her wrist tightened.

"Please, my lady, stay. Shipping logs are all very good and well, but they're also boring. They say this ship carried this cargo, or was lost on this date, but none say how the ship was lost."

Margareta shrugged. Ships were lost. Such

was the fate of men who thought to control the ocean. She yanked out of his grip and glared at him.

To her surprise, he looked suitably contrite. "I'm sorry if I hurt you, my lady. It's just that I don't know your name and if I didn't catch you, I would lose my chance for another day. You see, your father promised me an assistant, but all he seems to want to give me is you." He caught the anger in his eyes. "Not that the books you've found for me haven't been a great help – they have, I swear. It's just that I want to know more, and you are the only other person who comes here. As the lady of the house, I'm sure you know who I should ask for help instead?"

Margareta considered sweeping out of the room, but the pleading look in his eyes plucked at her heart in such a way that she relented. She perched on a bench, placed her hands on her lap, and lifted her eyebrows in mute query. What exactly did he want to know?

He leaned forward. "You see, I want to know why the ships were lost. Was it storms? Pirates? A battle with enemy ships? Sea monsters?"

Margareta bit her lip, wishing she could laugh. What would the ambassador say if he knew that she was the only kind of monster that lived in the sea? She shrugged again.

"Have you ever seen a sea monster?" he asked eagerly. "I've heard some of them can take the form of a beautiful woman who entices sailors to their deaths."

Margareta gasped – could he read her thoughts? Quickly, she schooled her expression into one of bewilderment, but it was too late. He'd seen her surprise.

"You have, haven't you?" he guessed. "I knew it! It is you. You're the same girl who was aboard the *Golden Eagle* when she sank. You're the girl who survived."

Margareta wished she could tell him what a fool he sounded, saying such things. She was the sea monster who had survived, not some weak-as-water maiden who needed to be rescued from the ocean, of all things. Her eyes narrowed. And how did he know such a thing, after all this time?

"I was the boy who was aboard the *Golden Eagle*, too," he continued. "We were in one of the ship's boats that made it to shore, except when I woke up, you were gone. I'm Erik." He held out his hand to her, palm up.

This ambassador was the squire? Margareta squinted at him, trying to see the boy in the well-built man before her. Maybe around the eyes and the mouth she could see a faint resemblance, but...

Her father had told her he'd searched for the boy, but found no trace of him anywhere on the island. It was as though he'd leaped back in the water to drown with the prince he'd served. Her father had suggested that the boy had never existed at all, until Margareta almost believed it. Sirens didn't suffer from the same maladies as sailors at sea for too long, though, so Margareta knew the boy had been real. So if he'd survived and this was him…that put him in a different light. He wasn't just some neighbouring king's ambassador. He was…a friend, of sorts. One she'd mourned who wasn't dead. Who wouldn't die here, no matter what she had to do to ensure it, Margareta swore.

She realised he'd continued speaking, and she shook her head, focussing on his words. Only her father knew she'd saved the squire, and he would never have told a soul, for it would mean telling people he had a siren for a daughter. So the only other people who knew were herself and the squire. He had to be the same boy.

"I had to go home to report Philip's death. My father was devastated at first, and then…well, there was so much to do. Learning to be a squire and one day a knight is one thing, but learning to be a prince, and politics, and how to rule a country…" Erik shook his head. "It's taken me this long to find my way back here, but I have to know. Do you have any books about sea monsters in these waters?"

All her parents' warnings about secrecy screamed at her to stop, and show the man nothing. And yet…something about him whispered to her that he was different – just as she'd known he was the day she saved him from the sea.

Perhaps it was time to find out what humans did know about her kind, so she could make sure they didn't learn more. Maybe they knew more than she gave them credit for. Her father certainly seemed to know plenty. Maybe he'd learned it all from a book in this very library. A book she could also learn from, so that one day she might manage to control her monstrous nature and not worry about how she might kill someone without meaning to. Maybe she could work out how not to kill Erik.

She regarded Erik for a long moment. He already owed her his life, if he truly was the squire she'd saved. Perhaps he could help her, and in some small way repay his debt.

Margareta winked at him, then set off for the section on myths and legends for the first time in what felt like forever.

Nineteen

Had she actually winked at him? The frosty maiden who hated him? Oh, not that she didn't have good reason to do so – she surely did, being forced to spend her time in the library with him instead of doing…whatever it was ladies did all day. Knit? Sew? Spin? He had no sisters and he could scarcely remember his mother, so Erik had never seen what highborn ladies did when no men were around. Surrounded by servants, they didn't need to do anything, but he couldn't imagine this girl sitting still and doing nothing for very long. She was as restless as the ocean. Erik had half expected her to open her mouth and shout at him a few times during their conversation, but she evidently took her vow of silence very seriously. In his memories, she was certainly no mute, and she understood him just fine, so her brothers must be very important to her.

And why not? They were family. Surely the girl loved her brothers, as all good girls did, and it would be a great loss to her whole family if they never returned from their holy crusade. Many others had perished, or disappeared, never to be heard from again, but he didn't dare say such things to her. The intelligence that shone through her eyes meant she probably already knew, and if she did not, he would not be cruel enough to tell her. Besides, she'd already worked one miracle when she saved him – another might not be as impossible for her as it would for ordinary people.

She returned with two leather buckets of

scrolls, that Erik helped her to set on the table. She unrolled the first one on the table, and Erik was mesmerised by the detailed drawing of a sea serpent, wrapping its massive coils around a sailing ship amid fierce waves. It was a monster, all right.

A fleeting image of blue scales on a creature easy as wide around as he himself, racing through the water beside him, passed through his mind, as if it was only yesterday he'd seen it. Had he seen a sea serpent? Is that what had brought him to the surface when he'd drowned? Or had the creature been a mermaid, like he'd dreamed? Whatever it had been, the creature had been doing the girl's bidding. That he knew for certain, for he'd heard her commanding the ocean itself. And a woman who could command the ocean in a world that relied on ships for trade was worth more than gold, jewels and the highest pedigree.

"Do you get many of these here?" he asked, trying to sound casual.

Her expression was impassive. Then she sighed.

She pulled a blank sheet of parchment toward her, picking up his quill with the ease of one who was familiar with writing, dipped it expertly in the ink, before scratching out the words:

Too cold. Serpents prefer warmer waters.

"Like most snakes," Erik mused. "But the ocean here is full of fish, and seals and maybe other creatures, too."

She nodded slowly. He got the impression she was waiting for him to continue.

Emboldened, he asked, "My lady, are there mermaids in these waters?"

The quill appeared in her fingers once more, flying across the parchment:

Don't be a fool. Mermaids don't exist outside of stories.

Her dark eyes held his. Mesmerising, that's what she was.

Would her gaze be equally cold if he kissed her?

Erik shook the idea from his head. If she was truly as powerful as he remembered, to kiss her would be to take his very life in his hands. But, by God, how much he wanted to. Even if it was the last thing he did, he would die a happy man.

She broke his gaze, turned on her heel, and marched out of the library.

Erik sighed. He'd been going so well, and then, like the bumbling fool he was, he'd made a mistake that sent her away again. But at least he'd managed to persuade her to show him some new scrolls that didn't mention a word of how many measures of wheat were aboard a ship when it sank.

Erik returned to the scrolls, which were filled with drawings that his eyes didn't see. Instead, his mind was fixed on her ocean-coloured eyes, and how they might light up if he kissed her.

Twenty

For the first time in his life, female voices arguing woke Erik. As his last dream faded, he realised he only heard one voice, but it was arguing loudly enough for two.

"I still don't see what you need me for. I am so close to getting the cloth right, I might have it finished this week. Instead, you want me to wake some man when you could easily do it yourself. You don't even need to touch him. Just throw a bucket of water over him, or whack him with a book, or…"

Erik jumped to his feet and met the annoyed gaze of the grey widow, who folded her arms across her chest.

"See?" the woman said. "He's awake. You don't need me. I'll go find someone to fetch food for him to break his fast."

A hand grasped the widow's sleeve, and Erik realised the girl stood behind her, using the widow for a shield. From him.

Pain smote his heart. "I'm sorry if I frightened you, my lady. The books you gave me yesterday were so interesting I stayed here late into the night to finish reading them. I must have fallen asleep on the table. My apologies if my snoring made you fear there was a monster in your library. I swear to you I mean you no harm. I am just a man."

The widow snorted. "Lady Margareta isn't frightened by much, sir. But a man who swears to do no harm had best keep his word, or evil will befall him. That I promise you."

Don't harm my charge or you will answer to me, Erik translated in his head.

"I spoke the truth. I mean her no harm. Both yourself and Lady Margareta are safe with me, Mistress…?"

"Lady Penelope," the widow supplied. She offered her hand, and Erik kissed it lightly. She lowered her voice so that only he could hear. "You should probably shave before you kiss her. She's not used to stubble."

Erik's hand flew to his face. Sure enough, he did need to shave. Muttering something about needing to wash, he hurried back to his chamber.

Twenty-One

Penelope's disapproval weighted heavily on Margareta. Penelope simply didn't understand the risks inherent in what Margareta was. If she touched the man, she could harm him.

"You danced with him just fine at the Harvest Ball,"," Penelope said. "Touched his hand and everything, so don't tell me there wasn't skin contact. And if he really is the boy you knew all those years ago, you definitely didn't hurt him then."

Margareta shook her head. Penelope could

never understand. She was human, and –

"So are you!" Penelope exploded. "As human as I am! All right, you swim more often than most, but what's a little magic, when it's in your blood? There is no law that says you're not allowed to love, or touch people or…do any of the things normal people do! How many people have you killed?"

Margareta knew as well as Penelope did that the answer was none.

"You've saved one man's life, and killed no one. That makes you pretty safe to be around, in my opinion. Why don't you just let things happen the way they should, and worry about the consequences later?" Penelope asked.

If one of the consequences was Erik's death, Margareta didn't want to just let things happen. She wanted to protect him, not kill him.

"Well, he wants to protect you almost as much as he wants to kiss you, so that's a good start," Penelope said.

Kiss her? He wanted more than that. He

wanted what every man wanted, Margareta was certain.

"Perhaps," Penelope said, "but that's not what he keeps thinking about. Not even what he dreams about. The only thing I've seen in his thoughts is visions of him kissing you. His eyes are fixed on your face. Except for the moment he first saw you, when he looked at your whole body, his focus is your eyes. Apparently, that's how you'll tell him whether his kiss is as perfect as he plans it to be."

A perfect kiss? Was there such a thing? The very idea intrigued Margareta. What would it be like to press her lips against Erik's and…

NO!

Margareta forced the thought from her mind. A kiss could lead to more and it was immodest to have such desires. If her father knew, he would only say it was her siren nature coming to the fore. No human girl would have such desires.

"Your father is a prude. Most girls dream about their first kiss, the same way he does about you. You could do worse, you know," Penelope said.

Of course she could. She could kill him.

"Just as long as you get the kind of kiss other girls only dream about first," Penelope said. "He'd die happy, you know. He's afraid of you, and that's one of the things he tells himself to bolster his courage. That if he died after kissing you, he would die happy."

No he wouldn't, Margareta thought angrily. He would die screaming, because sirens enjoyed the pain of their victims. She would —

"Now I'll go see that some breakfast is sent up, and leave you two alone," Penelope said, striding out of the library as Erik entered it. "And if she doesn't let you kiss her before I return, I'll see that the whole island knows she's an ill-mannered sea-cow!" she threw over her shoulder before vanishing from sight.

Margareta's face grew beet red.

Erik took pity on her embarrassment. "My apologies, my lady. Despite our history together, we have not been properly introduced. Allow me to correct this terrible oversight. I am Prince Erik, and I am honoured to meet you, Lady Margareta. Never have I met such a fair lady, who is also a graceful dancer and a learned scholar. I am quite entranced." He held out his hand.

A hand Margareta knew she should cover with her own. Custom demanded it. So did Penelope, who would know if she did not. She'd touched him before, as both a human and a siren, and he was still alive. If she could control herself for a few brief seconds, he would live to see tomorrow, too.

Margareta stretched out her arm, biting her lip as she saw her fingers shaking. If only she didn't have to touch him. She didn't want to hurt him. She wanted…

Erik captured her trembling fingers and brought them to his lips. Warm and soft, his lips made her fingers tingle as he kissed each one. Her mind screamed at her to pull away, but Margareta could not. Her own lips parted as she stared at him, eager to know what he would do next.

"Lady Penelope was right to berate me for being so unkempt. I was so caught up in my research, I forgot myself. Now, perhaps, I am in a fit state to greet you as I should have on the day we met. If I meet with your approval, then perhaps..." Erik swallowed, then lifted her hand to his now smooth cheek. "If my lady would permit, I would like to offer you a kiss of peace."

As her father's vassals offered to him, Margareta knew, and the captains who sought his favour. It was a religious thing, a chaste thing, a ceremony of power. It shouldn't send her heart racing like hers did now.

And yet...to refuse would be churlish. He honoured her, for such gestures were for leaders like her father. Not his youngest daughter.

Shakily, Margareta gave a nod.

Erik lifted his hands to touch her shoulders.

A fountain of butterflies erupted in her belly. This was dangerous, she shouldn't...

Margareta brought her other hand to his cheek so that she could cup his face. She took a deep, steadying breath, then stretched up to lay her lips against his.

For one brief moment, their kiss was a chaste thing. Then Margareta forgot everything but the feel of Erik against her, the taste of his mouth and the hardness of him between her thighs as he pulled her closer, closer, still kissing her as if she was the very air he needed to breathe. She needed more than air from him, more than the deep, gasping breaths she drew in as she tugged at his tunic, sliding her hands inside to feel soft skin over firm muscles, stroking every bit of him she could reach until she wrapped her fingers around the hardest part between them and –

Her eyes on fire with desire, Margareta met Erik's gaze. God, he wanted her as much as she wanted him. She wanted, oh how much she wanted…

"Oh God, Margareta, I love you," he groaned.

Love? What she would do to him wasn't love. Hers wasn't a kiss of peace. It was a kiss of death.

Margareta tore herself away from him and ran.

Twenty-Two

Erik buried his head in his hands. He shouldn't have said it. Shouldn't have admitted that he'd loved her for years, since they first met in the boat, because no girl could ever compare to her. And turning a kiss of peace into one of raging lust with a woman who was already frightened of him…he deserved to be scourged for such blasphemy. No wonder the girl had run.

But the feel of her hands on him, stroking him in exactly the right way, as if she was as overcome by her own feelings as he was by his…

No. He'd imagined it, surely. No woman in creation would be so bold. A woman who could control the ocean could certainly control herself.

Whereas he was…an uncontrolled mess.

Cursing himself, Erik set off to find some cold water to douse his desire.

Twenty-Three

Margareta slammed the door behind her, then put her back to it, breathing hard. She wasn't sure if it was because she'd sprinted from the library to Penelope's chambers or whether it was the strange siren heat that still coursed through her that made her heart beat so fast within her chest that she could scarcely catch her breath.

"That good, was he?" Penelope asked calmly, wetting the end of her thread before inserting it through the eye of her needle. "I would have thought you'd have taken your time, but it's hard to savour your first."

Margareta tried to calm the jumble of images in her head so that Penelope would understand, for no one could be so calm in the face of what she had just experienced.

"I remember the day I first kissed Godfrey," Penelope said dreamily, as if she wasn't paying attention to Margareta at all. "We'd met at some of my father's feasts, but I'd never been able to exchange more than a few words with him. He'd told all sorts of stories about war and what he'd seen, stories I could listen to for hours, but my father never allowed me near enough to tell him so. But our eyes met across the hall enough times for him to start seeking me out, or find excuses to visit my father at home. One day, he brought an urgent message for my father when he was out, and only I was home. As was proper, I offered him refreshments, and suggested he wait for my father. He paid me some pretty compliment about how he'd wait forever for me, or some such thing, and he stumbled over the words as he never had in his stories. That's when he first kissed me. Well, I pushed him against the wall and kissed him, actually. Didn't take more than a moment before he was kissing me back just as eagerly. We kissed for quite a while, long enough for him to get good and excited so I could assess the goods, so to speak, which I admit were quite impressive, before my father's arrival interrupted us. The bustle at the door was enough for us to straighten our clothing and for me to whisper an invitation to meet me in the garden later that night, and the rest, well..." Penelope laughed. "By morning, I wanted no other man for my husband. Though from the way that man looks at you, he might be cut from the same cloth. My advice is to make sure he's as good with his hands as he is with his mouth before you agree to more. A good lover should give more pleasure than he receives."

Margareta's mouth hung open. Penelope had to be jesting, surely. No woman...

"No woman wants a bad lover," Penelope finished for her. "I'd rather join the nunnery permanently than share a bed with a man who doesn't absolutely adore me, or at least love me."

A fleeting memory of her mother's people, and what they did to men who didn't please them, fluttered through Margareta's mind. She didn't want to see sharks devour Erik. She liked him. At least a little. He spoke to her face instead of her chest, and seemed to care what she thought. No one else except Penelope did that — not even her father. All he cared about was getting his sons back, her bawdy brothers who would go back to their violent ways the moment they regained human form, she was certain of it. At least she could save the people of Beacon Isle from them, if the island belonged to her. Or her husband, which was almost the same thing.

"Your brothers don't deserve the sacrifice you're making for them," Penelope said sadly. "But the prince you left in the library? Why don't you give him a chance to show you what kind of husband he'd make?"

Margareta regarded Penelope for a long moment. She might not want to admit it, but her friend was right. Her brothers didn't deserve what she was doing for them, but that didn't matter. She had given her word, and the people of Beacon Isle would suffer if she broke it.

But if she hadn't given her word…then she could speak to Erik, and tell him why he couldn't possibly be in love with a sea monster, for that's what she was to him. A creature in a book that sank ships and killed the prince she now knew was his brother. Who could kill him just as easily if she lost control and gave in to her siren nature.

One thing was certain: she didn't want Erik to suffer his brother's fate. She didn't want to watch a man she knew and perhaps even liked be ripped apart by sharks.

Never mind that she'd wanted to rip his clothes off earlier. It was a small miracle she hadn't ripped off his head, or any other part of him.

Margareta turned on her heel and left the room. She knew what she had to do.

There was only one thing that would stop her from turning into the most lascivious siren ever to step out of the sea: immersing herself in the ocean for a swim. Surely that would cool her desire.

She hurried down the stone steps to the now deserted great hall, making her way out the gate with her head held high to forestall any questions. None of the guards would dare stop her – they knew who she was.

A flock of ravens flapped over the high walls of her father's house as she left its shelter, but Margareta paid them no heed. The only ravens she cared about were her brothers, and as long as she maintained her silence, she was doing all she could for them.

Her private cove was empty, as it should be. Margareta lost no time in removing her clothing – all of it, this time.

The waves kissed her skin as she trudged through the sand, until the water reached her waist. Then she lost all pretence of humanity and shifted into her true form, extending her fins past what had been her toes as cool skin enveloped her legs, turning them into a powerful tail as blue as the deep ocean waters where she was headed.

Twenty-Four

Erik splashed himself with cold water until the ewer was empty, before he dressed and headed to the highest part of the house, the passage that looked out over White Harbour to the sea. The waves were as turbulent as his own thoughts today. Though he hated to admit it, he had the answer his father sought: Beacon Isle paid tribute to no one, for it had no lord or monarch aside from its Master, who was a rich man indeed. The contents of his father's treasury were nothing to the port duties Master

Nicholas collected in a single year.

Beacon Isle would be a rich prize to anyone who could conquer it, but the very nature of the island made it near impregnable. Master Nicholas had a neat navy of merchant ships that could turn to war as easily as they did to trade. Erik's father would never win the island by force.

And so he lingered here, pursuing his real quest — twin quests, truly. His pursuit of the mythical creatures who had saved him, and the girl who commanded them. A girl who drove him to insanity, so that he kissed her and professed his love in the most awkward way.

No wonder she'd left, undoubtedly disgusted that he would do such a thing.

He must have imagined her hands on him.

Even just the thought of it heated his blood to boiling again. Erik cursed and headed back to his chamber for more water. No, he'd go to the sea for a swim. Immersing his whole body in cold water would be a much better idea.

He reached the stairs, then stopped when he

heard voices. Male voices this time.

"Did you see her again last night?"

"I see her most every night. She swims into the shallows in that cove just past the breakwater, lays herself down on the sand, and sleeps."

"Why haven't you taken her for your own if she's so pretty, then?"

"Oh, she's pretty enough, but she's a mermaid, man. What use is a woman who has a tail where her legs should be? Waste of a pair of tits if she has no legs to dive between."

"I heard of a brave man who tamed a mermaid once. They say she was the sweetest lay who ever lived, and she was his, because he tamed her. See, the trick is to stop her going back to the ocean — she's powerless on land. What he did was cut off her tail, I heard. Not like you would with a fish. No, she's got legs beneath those fins, and if you want to get between them, you have to cut her legs free. Do that, and she'll be your slave for life."

"A man took a sword to a mermaid and

lived to tell the tale?"

"On my honour, though I heard it was just a knife. And the man was no ordinary man, but the Master of Beacon Isle himself."

"The Master? Master Nicholas?"

"Maybe. Might explain that daughter of his. Proud and beautiful as the day is long, not like normal girls. Wouldn't surprise me if she was half mermaid."

The other man laughed. "But which half? Now we know why the Master hasn't married her off yet."

"Maybe. Hey, when does she come ashore? Maybe I should try my luck, if mermaids are such sweet wives."

"Just after sunset."

At sunset he could see a mermaid? Without hesitation, Erik took the stairs three at a time, but he saw no sign of the men who had spoken. Only a pair of ravens perched on the window ledge, which flew off as he approached. Never mind, he told himself. If he could see a real mermaid with his own eyes, he could show the creature to Margareta. Then she might trust him with her secrets, or at least stop thinking he was a fool.

He felt for his knife, closing his fingers reassuringly around the hilt. A mermaid was a wild creature at best, and all the stories agreed on one thing: she would kill him without hesitation if she felt threatened. The knife was for his protection.

Twenty-Five

Erik reached the breakwater, and only when he stood on it could he see the small cove he'd heard the men speak about. Small, private, and empty. On a hot summer's day, he'd love to take a dip in the water himself. Now, though, he had no intention of entering the sea. Not if a mermaid lurked close by.

Feeling like a coward, he climbed a tree, hoping its branches would hide him from sight. None of his research suggested that mermaids could climb trees, but Erik didn't let himself feel too secure on his perch. Research and myths were one thing, but facing a mermaid in the flesh was something different entirely.

For what felt like forever, Erik clung to his branch, watching and waiting. He'd spot a shadow in the waves, only to realise it was a piece of seaweed or flotsam. His eyes began to grow heavy as he squinted into the sun, straining for even a glimpse of the mythical mermaid.

When she did appear, he almost missed it. A wave washed further up the beach than its fellows and when it retreated, it left behind what Erik at first thought was the decoration from the bow of a ship. A stylised fish-woman, stretching her arms and her breasts before her while her tail fanned out behind.

And then….she moved, flicking a piece of seaweed off her tail, before she combed her fingers through her dark hair.

Erik almost fell out of his tree. A mermaid. A real mermaid, not fifty feet from him!

With care to make as little sound as possible, he climbed down, creeping through the shrubbery to get a better look at the mythical creature he'd sought for so long.

Slowly, slowly, he raised his head above a bush. He saw her dark hair, then the pale skin of her back, and his breath caught in his throat. Legs. She stood on two legs, just like him, though hers were bare.

In one moment, she'd shredded half the tales he'd read about her kind. Erik grinned. He'd write his own book, perhaps, and give Master Nicholas' library a copy. Or give it to Lady Margareta as a gift. Now that was an idea.

He should have asked Margareta to come with him to see the mermaid. Tomorrow he'd bring her to the cove and watch her reaction.

He must have made some sound, because the mermaid suddenly stiffened. She scanned the cove, then turned around and directed her piercing gaze at the bushes where Erik hid. His instincts screamed at him to duck, to get out of sight, but he was mesmerised by the woman before him. And she was a woman. Mermaid or not, the goddess who stood on the sand had two shapely legs, a flat belly and a pair of breasts he ached to touch.

The siren had him under her spell, his fuzzy mind told him, but Erik waved the thought away. Who cared? She was beautiful and alluring and everything a man could want. Everything he could ever want.

Erik rose to his feet and stepped out of hiding. He narrowed the distance between them and held out his arms. When she pressed her cold body against his, he closed his arms around her, and knew nothing but the bliss of holding his heart's desire.

Twenty-Six

Margareta let the wave carry her up the beach, then stretched out on the sand as the water retreated. Perhaps she'd swum a little too far today, after so long on land. She should swim more regularly, instead of spending so much time with Penelope and Melitta, or in the library. That would keep her away from Erik, too, which could only be a good thing for both of them.

Slowly, she let her body transform from tail to legs once more. Life was so much simpler under the sea. But without her tail, she most certainly felt the chill in the evening air, so she couldn't stay here for long. She'd need to dress and head back up to her father's house before dark, or her father's guards would shut the gate. They'd open it for her if she commanded it with an imperious wave in the absence of words, but her father would hear of it, and no good would come of that. At the least, she'd receive a long lecture about how she shouldn't give in to her siren and swim. More like he didn't want her messing with the ships approaching the harbour before they'd paid their duties. He never mentioned ships that had recently left the harbour, though. Maybe he didn't care about those.

Margareta flicked her hair, running her fingers through it to free it from some of the tangles.

A gasp from behind her made her whirl on the spot, looking for the hidden watcher. Had he seen her tail? Had he seen her transform? If anyone told her father…

No one would tell her father, for none would live to tell tales, Margareta resolved. She sent out a silent call, whispering through the trees where she was certain someone hid. No man was immune to a siren's call.

A man stepped out of the shadows, stumbling across the sand to obey her call. One man, no more.

He held out his arms, eyes begging for an embrace. For death's embrace.

Margareta stepped into the circle of Erik's arms and looked into his eyes. Though she might look like a human, all her siren senses were awakened. If you love me, show me, she silently commanded him.

He nodded, and brought his lips to hers for a kiss. Her lips warmed at his touch, wanting more. If she could have spoken, she would have said so. As it was, she let her eyes speak for her.

Erik's hand stroked her leg, trailing his fingers higher until he reached the junction of her thighs. Margareta gasped as his fingers slid inside, stroking her even more intimately than before.

"I love you," he whispered, tightening his grip around her with one arm as her knees weakened from the caresses from his other hand. His gaze held hers as he did something with his fingers that sent waves of pleasure washing over her.

Margareta opened her mouth in a silent scream of joy, while Erik's fingers moved within her again.

When the next tide of pleasure swept through her, Margareta forgot caution and secrecy and all the things that might make her stop. She tore at Erik's clothes, pushing him to the sand. She would have him, and silly human social conventions meant nothing.

For the first time in her life, Margareta lost control as she surrendered to her siren.

Twenty-Seven

Margareta woke slowly, revelling in the unaccustomed warmth of her bed. She must have fallen asleep on the sand in her tail again. She'd best turn back to human and get some clothing on before some fisherman stumbled across her.

She blinked away the sleep from her eyes, stretching. Her legs touched warm flesh and cloth. Margareta tried to jerk away from the other body, but a heavy arm lay across her, holding her close.

By all the saints, who had she killed?

She squirmed out from under the man and flipped him over. She almost cried with relief when she saw his chest rise as he drew breath. She hadn't killed him. Hesitantly, she reached for the cloak that shrouded him and pulled the fabric away from his face.

Margareta staggered back, falling to the sand.

Erik. She'd surrendered to her siren nature and seduced Erik.

Now, more than ever, she wished she could speak to him. Damn her stupid brothers for getting cursed, and twice damn her father for persuading her to break their curse. It was almost as bad as being cursed herself, and what had she done to deserve it?

She stared down at Erik. If what her father told her was true, she might have permanently damaged Erik. She wouldn't know until he woke whether he'd been driven mad by whatever she'd done to him.

Seven hells…what had she done to him?

She'd never allowed a man close enough to her for something like this to happen before. A small part of her whispered that now she'd tried intimacy with a man, she would want plenty more, but Margareta hushed it. If her pleasure came at the cost of Erik's sanity, it was too high a price to pay. Ever.

Margareta shook Erik, but he didn't wake. Her heart sank. If he'd lost his senses, he might never wake. Killing him would be a mercy, and it would be her responsibility to end the suffering she had inflicted on him.

She was a true siren. She'd destroyed a man, and nothing could fix this.

"Whore!" screamed a voice, as something sharp hit her shoulder.

Margareta whirled, and something hit her back.

"Could have saved us, but a whore like you couldn't stay a maiden for long enough!" shrieked another voice.

"Whore!" hissed a third as dark projectiles hit her on both sides.

This time, Margareta saw one of them. It wasn't a projectile at all, but a dark bird that darted down to peck at Erik. Margareta flapped a hand at the bird to shoo it away from her unconscious lover, but she was too late — its beak was already red with blood.

For the second time in two days, Margareta lost control of her human nature. But this time, the siren reigned supreme.

The ocean surged up the beach at her command, circling her and Erik with an army of waves while the sand beneath him remained untouched.

Suddenly the air was filled with dark feathers as half a dozen ravens flew in to attack Margareta from all sides. She directed the water to fight them, but it wasn't enough — some of them reached her, clawing and pecking at her face before she managed to stun one with her fist. She only had a moment's reprieve, though, before the stunned bird was replaced with two more, angrier and more intent on drinking her blood than their disoriented brother.

All the while, their caws sounded more like cries of "Whore!" than the calls of ordinary birds.

One of them fastened onto a chunk of her hair, beating its wings furiously as it tried to rip the hair from her head. If she could have made a sound, Margareta would have screamed, it hurt so much when the lock of hair parted from her scalp. She felt something warm against her back and spun around, terrified that it was a cascade of her own blood. Instead, she found Erik, risen to his feet with murder in his eyes.

"I won't let them hurt you," he vowed, brandishing a knife. A bird darted toward Margareta, then changed direction, aiming for Erik's eyes. His arm whipped out, swifter than a bird in flight. Light flashed on his blade as he separated the bird from its head, and both fell at Margareta's feet. "I count ten more. Keep doing whatever you're doing, and leave killing them to me."

Margareta nodded, not sure what to think. The only clear thought in her head was that Erik had most certainly not lost his wits, and whatever she and Erik had done last night, he hadn't paid the price for it.

She punched another bird as it dived for her, sending it into the crest of a wave, which quickly sucked it under. Concentrating on the water, she built up a particularly big wave and used it to engulf three more birds. Panting, she lifted her arm to clout another, only to see Erik cut it down before it could reach her.

"That's all of them, my lady," Erik said, sounding just as breathless as she.

Margareta turned to face him. Erik was as naked as she was, except for the cloak he'd wrapped around them both while they lay on the beach.

Memories trickled back of their night together, two bodies so entwined even she hadn't known which limbs belonged to who. Nor had she cared. He might be her first, but no other man could compare. And not only had she not killed him, but she'd chosen to protect him even in the throes of unbridled passion. Somehow, Erik had succumbed to her siren call and lived. That made him a very special man indeed. Perhaps Penelope was right about him.

Staring into Erik's eyes, she felt lost.

Margareta dismissed the ocean, so that she stood alone with Erik on the damp sand.

He chuckled. "My lady, you should probably cover yourself. Looking like that, you could charm the birds from the sky as well as the fish from the sea." As he wrapped his cloak around her, he winked.

It took Margareta a moment to realise what he'd seen. Not just her naked body, but her power over the ocean. Her blood ran cold, colder even than when she swam the depths as a mermaid. Had he seen…?

"I heard rumours of a mermaid, and I came to spy the truth of it for myself before bringing you to the cove so that you might see the creature. Only to find…you know far more of such things than I ever will." Erik pulled her close, laying his cheek beside hers so that his lips brushed her ear. "Marry me, my lady of the seas. I will love you and keep your secrets as long as I live, and all I ask in return is your love, if you are willing."

Margareta wanted to shout her answer at the top of her lungs, but her silence stole her voice, even as her lips formed a YES.

"Whore!" screeched a voice. "Faithless woman! How dare you take this man into your bed while we suffer. The man who killed your own brothers. Neither of you deserve to live!"

To Margareta's stunned horror, a raven with an injured wing hopped across the sand to attack her feet, screaming obscenities and accusations.

A firm hand grasped the bird by the neck and held it up in the air. "You're a fool, Corbin. I gave you and your brothers a chance to live, to atone for your crimes. I even told you how to break the curse. You couldn't get girls to fall in love with you, but your sister, whose loyalty to her family made her vow to save you, still might have freed you. If you'd waited a few more hours, she would have broken the spell with seven years of silence, virgin or no. But now…you have forfeited your right to even a sister's love." The woman who'd spoken wrung the neck of the bird and tossed it on the sand beside the other piles of damp feathers that Margareta now realised were the corpses of the rest of the ravens.

Her brothers.

The woman bit down hard on her lip, raising her hands high. The birds moved, floating until their bodies formed a line on the sand. Only then did they begin to lose their feathers, growing until they became not birds but young men. Young men she remembered, though they were older now. Raban had been a boy of her own age when she last saw him, the youngest of her brothers, and now he was a man grown. A man decapitated, too, for his head lay a foot from his body.

Margareta let out a sob, and another. The

sound of her voice seemed to echo in the cove, for it had been so long since she had heard it. "I didn't want them to die!" she cried, falling to her knees.

The same strong hand that had wrung Corbin's neck landed on her shoulder. "Then you are a better person than any of your brothers. They would have killed you, and your boy here." The woman nodded at Erik. "He'll make a better Master of the island than any of your kin."

"But Father," Margareta began, horrified anew at the thought of what her father would say when he saw his precious sons laid low like this. They had died, while she yet lived. "Father is Master here. He will never forgive me for this, and Erik…"

"I summoned him to the cove when I arrived. He is already on his way," the woman said.

Sure enough, Father limped onto the sand, leaning heavily on his stick. He looked so frail now, as though the seven years which had passed were seventy instead. "What do you want, witch?" he demanded. "First you take my sons from me, sending them far away, and now you think to take my daughter, too?"

"I am Mistress Kun, no mere witch, and you would do well to address me so, Nicholas," the woman said. "Your sons sealed their own fate seven years ago, and today, they demonstrated that they have no right to live among decent people. They died at the hands of a woman. I call it justice."

"My sons?" Father faltered.

Mistress Kun pointed at the bodies, hidden from Father's sight by a sandbank.

It seemed to take him forever to reach the top, and when he did, his expression changed from bewilderment to something Margareta didn't think looked entirely human. His lips peeled away from his teeth and his eyes grew wild.

"What have you done to my sons?" he howled. His gaze fixed on Margareta. "It was you! A whore like your mother, opening your legs to every pretty man you can find. I might not have managed to kill your slut of a mother, but I will deal with you!" He advanced on Margareta, who cried out in fear, unable to move. He managed to take three steps before he keeled over face first on the sand.

Margareta wanted to dash forward to help him to his feet, but she remained rooted to the spot. Had her father really threatened to kill her? Or tried to kill her mother?

Mistress Kun knelt down to examine Father. "Dead," she grunted as she rose from her crouch. "Good riddance, too. You two will make a better job of ruling this place."

Two? Margareta stared at Erik, who looked as bewildered as she felt.

"My father sent me here to find a way to bring Beacon Isle into his kingdom. I was to discover which king the Master owed fealty to, and persuade him to become a part of my father's kingdom instead. Master Nicholas would not agree, but perhaps his heir..." Erik cleared his throat. "Lady Margareta, when your father's heir becomes Master of this island, perhaps you would be willing to put in a good word for me, and arrange a meeting?"

Heir? With her brothers dead and their curse broken, her father's heir would be…her.

"Marry me," she said.

Erik laughed. "I intend to, if you'll let me."

Margareta shook her head. "No, marry me. Beacon Isle belongs to me, and to my husband. Marry me and you may have the island." She gazed at Erik. "I ask only one thing."

"Name it," Erik urged.

Margareta wet her lips. "That you love me every night of your life as you did last night."

"I will," Erik vowed.

Mistress Kun cackled. "Sounds like happily ever after to me." She waved at the bodies lined up along the beach. "I will see that everyone knows the boys died far from home and when your father found out, he died of grief. You will inherit, no matter what his wishes were. You are the last of his line now."

She gave a little bow to Margareta.

Enchantresses did nothing without a price. "I thank you, Mistress Kun," she said steadily. "How may I repay you for all that you have done for me?"

"For us," Erik corrected.

Kun grinned. "He's right, and I'll ask a favour of you both. Take Melitta and her mother with you when you leave the island. And when you are dowager queen, return to the isle and rule until your grandson comes of age to inherit the position of Master."

"It will be done," Erik vowed, and Margareta nodded, forgetting that she now had the use of her voice.

"A blessing on you both," Kun said gravely, waving her hand in their direction. "May you have your happily ever after as long as you both shall live." And with that, she disappeared.

Erik turned to Margareta. "Is this truly what you want? Will you be happy?"

For the first time in seven years, Margareta

laughed aloud. "You already owe me your life, squire. I know you'll make me happy. I only hope I can return the favour."

"You already do," Erik said fervently. "And you always will."

Author's Note

If you're looking for more fairy tale retellings…here's a sneak peek from *Awaken: Sleeping Beauty Retold*, the next book in the series.

Bonus Sneak Peek

Awaken: Sleeping Beauty Retold

"You should be here, planning a coronation ceremony and ruling the kingdom. Not riding about, chasing birds in the woods!" Lady Schutz hissed.

Lord Siward sighed. "Grandmother, this kingdom is so small, it almost rules itself. And it has been scarcely three weeks since the king died. The earth has not even had time to settle over his grave. It would be an insult to his memory to attempt to steal his throne before we know whether an heir can be found."

"Normal kingdoms name a new king on the same day the old one dies. A kingdom should not be without a ruler for even a day!" she insisted.

"If only our kingdom could be normal, but it is not. Neither is it without a ruler. I am not leaving the kingdom. I am simply riding out of the city for a little while. I shall visit the borders and the outlying villages, make sure all is well, and if I choose to spend a day or two hawking, what of it? It is the sport of kings, after all, and you are so set on me becoming one. It seems to me I should enjoy some of the privileges, seeing as I already shoulder the burdens of a position which are not mine to bear."

She threw her wrinkled hands up into the air. "Be it on your own head, then, if some other noble tries to claim the throne while you are playing with birds!"

"If some madman attempts it, then he is welcome to the throne," Lord Siward snapped. If only another man would lay claim to that much-vaunted chair, then he could do the job his father had done, instead of trying to rule in the king's stead. If they could find an heir…

But there was no heir. The king and queen had managed to have one child, and she had died young. A normal kingdom could ask for a near relation who had married into one of the royal families of a neighbouring kingdom, but this was no normal kingdom.

So that left him. Siward sighed, knowing he would have to ascend the throne on his return. No other man in court was capable of ruling, though others had blood far more noble than his. Yet the king on his deathbed had appointed him regent, for his sins.

All the more reason to take this trip now, for it might be his last chance at freedom before the heavy yoke of kingship settled on his shoulders.

His head started to clear as he left the city. Perhaps it was the lack of courtly arse-kissing, or maybe it was the clean scent from the woods instead of the smoke from cookfires, but he took heart when the city walls vanished from sight.

It was easily a week's ride to the border by way of the main road, but checking the borders was his first task. Every year, like his father and grandfather before him, Siward rode the borders, checking for signs of weakness. He hadn't found one yet, but if ever there was a time he needed one…it was now.

When he arrived at the end of the road, Siward sighed. He hadn't expected any change, though he had hoped for one.

Bramble hedges soared into the sky, forming a wall more formidable than simple stone. This wall ringed the kingdom, allowing no one in or out, and it had stood since his grandfather's time. His grandfather, Lord Schutz, had said the Wall had been a simple hedge once, but when the princess passed, the plants had risen up in protest to protect the kingdom. Siward never understood what they protected the kingdom from, for his grandfather had rambled considerably in his old age. Sometimes, he'd said it was to prevent a plague. At other times, he'd insisted it was to prevent war with a neighbouring kingdom, who had apparently killed the princess.

The truth of the tale was lost in time – and with his grandfather, who had lain in his grave for many years now.

Yet the Wall still stood, testament to some mysterious truth. Perhaps someone had cursed the kingdom, Siward decided. It seemed as good an explanation as any. But if it weren't for the Wall, he could send messengers to neighbouring kingdoms to search for an heir. With it…he would be king.

The first time he'd seen the Wall, Siward had slashed at it with his sword, determined like a hundred other men before him that he could cut his way through. The brambles would have none of it, wrapping tendrils around his sword until they dragged it from his hand as they repaired the damage to the Wall as though he had never sliced a single stroke. The Wall was magic, most certainly. Which made it all the harder for a soldier like himself to understand. There were no witches in the kingdom, so whoever had cast it must be on the other side of the Wall, and out of his reach.

Astor, his hunting hawk, ruffled her feathers as if impatient to do something more than sit on her perch.

"You have the right of it, my friend," Siward told the bird, pulling off the creature's hood. "Let us hunt, and forget politics for a time. Worrying about it will not bring down the Wall."

He headed off the road, toward a spot known only to his family. It had the best hawking in the kingdom, and so it would continue as long as its location remained a closely-kept secret. Not even his grandmother knew this spot, he'd wager, for she had no desire to hunt.

He unhooded Astor, held his fist high in the air, and watched the bird fly off with powerful wingbeats. Siward wished for a moment that he could fly with her, high above the Wall, to see the world outside. Was it so different to their kingdom? As long as the Wall stood, he would never know.

With his eyes on Astor, Siward urged his horse to follow the bird. The forest was not so dense here, though there was no village nearby. Perhaps there once had been one, but it had been too close to the border that before the Wall it had been attacked too many times until it had been abandoned. Surely there would have been some ruins left, then, to mark where the town had stood. Yet Siward had never seen them. Perhaps the brambles and briars had consumed those, too.

Astor hovered, and Siward held his breath for a moment before the hawk dived, gracefully seizing a bird on the wing before her prey had even been aware of her presence.

Astor swooped down with her catch still in her talons, toward a briar-shrouded rock.

Siward thought she would perch on the rock, but Astor dipped down behind it and disappeared. Swearing, he rode around, trying to find the bird, but the rock seemed solid on all sides, and the bird was nowhere in sight. He called her and heard an answering cry, but she did not reappear.

He swore again. The rock must be hollow, and his bloody bird was in the middle of it. If he didn't catch her before she devoured her prey, he'd lose her as a hunting hawk. Bird be damned, but she was his best, and he was loath to lose her. If there was no other way in, he would have to climb.

Siward had not climbed rocks or trees since he was a boy, but he was not so old that he did not enjoy doing it again. Just as long as his grandmother or his future subjects didn't catch him behaving like a youth.

The rock had a surprising number of easy toeholds for him, so it wasn't long until Siward had reached the top. The view he saw from his vantage point, though, made his mouth fall open in surprise. What he had taken for a rock was in fact a sprawling building – he'd been climbing the walls. Astor, bright bird that she was, had perched on a wall that had partially fallen down, hiding her from his sight until now. He called her again, but the stubborn bird did not move.

Siward swore again. He would have to fetch her. At least it would be a simple matter of walking along the walls to her current spot, scooping her up and hooding her once more.

He could not keep his eyes on the bird and his footing, though, and by the time he looked up, the blasted bird had moved to a wall in the middle of the building. She teetered there for a moment, before diving into the room below.

Siward made his way to the spot where he'd last seen Astor, and stopped. Below him was a courtyard, free of the collapsed roof fragments most of the other rooms had sported. Yet it was not the courtyard that drew his eye, but the incredibly lifelike statue of a woman in the middle of it, surrounded by roses.

Made of alabaster or white marble, she looked as though she would open her eyes and rise at any moment. Some virgin goddess or the Queen of Heaven, Siward guessed, depending on how old the statue was. Yet it looked newly carved, not as though it had been lying in this ruin for centuries, as surely it had been. A wondrous work of art indeed.

If he had to take the throne, he would place this statue in the throne room, so that every time he was bored, he could stare at her and wonder what her story was, and remember how he'd found her on his last days of freedom.

Siward jumped down from the wall, bending his knees to cushion the impact of his landing. Good thing, too, for the ground beneath his feet was harder than he expected. Swiping his booted foot through the leaf litter, he pushed aside the thin layer to reveal a mosaic floor of remarkable craftsmanship, though it paled into insignificance when compared to the magnificent statue.

Now he was closer, she looked even more divine. Like his every desire made flesh – or stone, at least. Siward laughed at himself. A statue so real it stirred his loins. Perhaps becoming king would not be such a bad thing. He would be expected to take a queen, and ensure a clear succession. That would stop him from lusting after statues.

No, he decided, inspecting the goddess, for no real woman could look so perfect. He must have this statue in his throne room.

He reached out to touch the stone, to see what fastened her to the plinth below. Perhaps he could move her out of here and send someone to collect the statue, so that it would be in place when he returned. If she had been fastened by her feet and fallen over at some point, he might be able to…

A briar shot out, twining around his wrist so fast he could not move it. "What in blazes – " he began, only now realising that the plants had sent tendrils around both of his legs and his other arm, too. A thicker branch snaked around his middle, yanking him away from the statue.

Siward shouted for help, but he was alone in the ruin, as he well knew.

No, not quite alone.

Astor, his traitorous bird, landed on the plinth beside the statue's shoulder and peered at the goddess' face, as though working out what her lips would taste like. That beak could chip stone, and ruin the statue. The bird had caused enough trouble today.

"No!" Siward commanded. "Leave the girl alone. She is not to be harmed."

Finally deciding to be obedient, the bird flew off, perching on the wall once more.

Siward breathed a sigh of relief. She was safe.

He thought he heard something rustling through the leaves, and turned his attention back to the statue. What he saw stole his breath and his voice.

For the statue's closed eyes now stood open, green as emeralds, as she stared back at him.

The tale continues in the next book in the
series
Awaken:
Sleeping Beauty Retold

About the Author

Demelza Carlton has always loved the ocean, but on her first snorkelling trip she found she was afraid of fish.

She has since swum with sea lions, sharks and sea cucumbers and stood on spray drenched cliffs over a seething sea as a seven-metre cyclonic swell surged in, shattering a shipwreck below.

Demelza now lives in Perth, Western Australia, the shark attack capital of the world.

The *Ocean's Gift* series was her first foray into fiction, followed by her suspense thriller *Nightmares* trilogy. She swears the *Mel Goes to Hell* series ambushed her on a crowded train and wouldn't leave her alone.

Want to know more? You can follow Demelza on Facebook, Twitter, YouTube or her website, Demelza Carlton's Place at:

www.demelzacarlton.com

Books by Demelza Carlton

Ocean's Gift series

Ocean's Gift (#1)

Ocean's Infiltrator (#2)

Ocean's Depths (#3)

Water and Fire

Turbulence and Triumph series

Ocean's Justice (#1)

Ocean's Trial (#2)

Ocean's Triumph (#3)

Ocean's Ride (#4)

Ocean's Cage (#5)

Ocean's Birth (#6)

How To Catch Crabs

Nightmares Trilogy

Nightmares of Caitlin Lockyer (#1)

Necessary Evil of Nathan Miller (#2)

Afterlife of Alana Miller (#3)

Mel Goes to Hell series

Welcome to Hell (#1)
See You in Hell (#2)
Mel Goes to Hell (#3)
To Hell and Back (#4)
The Holiday From Hell (#5)
All Hell Breaks Loose (#6)

Romance Island Resort series

Maid for the Rock Star (#1)
The Rock Star's Email Order Bride (#2)
The Rock Star's Virginity (#3)
The Rock Star and the Billionaire (#4)
The Rock Star Wants A Wife (#5)
The Rock Star's Wedding (#6)
Maid for the South Pole (#7)
Jailbird Bride (#8)

The Complex series

Halcyon
Fishtail

www.ingramcontent.com/pod-product-compliance
Lightning Source LLC
Chambersburg PA
CBHW070953120726
47910CB00004B/1211